TEMPORARY HUSBAND

TEMPORARY HUSBAND

•

Patricia K. Azeltine

AVALON BOOKS
NEW YORK

PRINTED IN THE UNITED STATES OF AMERICA
ON ACID-FREE PAPER
BY HADDON CRAFTSMEN, BLOOMSBURG,
PENNSYLVANIA

To my father, Charles John Burian, who taught me how to work hard and never give up on my dreams.

Special thanks to Jean McCord, McCord Associates, for your excellent editing skills and encouragement, and my mentor, Frank Lambirth for imparting his experience and vast knowledge to me.

As always, thanks to my husband, Steve, and my daughters, Mary and Katie. You're my world, my everything!

Chapter One

*W*anted: *Temporary husband.*

Stacey Williams stared at the *South Sound Daily* newspaper want ads. What a mess she was in. What had she been thinking, blurting out to her parents that she had eloped? She hadn't dated in months, let alone met and married a man. For years her father had pressured her to get married and have a child, a third-generation heir to the Williams fortune. Little did her father know that finding a husband was harder than it looked, especially when she had no interest in marriage. Why couldn't he accept the fact that her career came first?

But now that the doctors had found a

suspicious growth in her father, he had started pushing more intensely. She couldn't disappoint him now, not when he needed her most.

She peered at the calendar on the faded orange partition in her cubicle and drummed her fingers on the heavy wood desk. Her parents were throwing her a wedding reception this coming weekend. She had five days to find a man to pose as her husband.

Once more, Stacey read the *Help Wanted* section—a column so tiny in this small-town newspaper that if she blinked she might have missed it. *Wanted: Temporary husband. Reasonable pay. Easy work. Inquire through newspaper.*

Stacey groaned. Would anyone take her seriously? Would anyone apply? What would she do if no one did? She needed an alternate plan, but what? She could never tell her father that she had lied to him. He wanted her married, and that was that. What Stan Williams wanted, Stan Williams got. He wasn't a man to sit around and wait for anything, not even a grandchild. Stacey wondered if he would find a way to rush nine months of pregnancy.

She glanced at a family photograph of her father, mother, two sisters, and herself. Fate had a funny way of twisting lives around. Her father had everything money could buy: a successful computer business, a huge home in the San Juan Islands, a penthouse condo in downtown Seattle, a loving wife, and three adoring daughters. But what he wanted most was a grand-child—preferably a grandson. Stacey's older sister, Faith, had chosen a spiritual career and become a nun, and her younger sister, Pamela, couldn't have children.

That left Stacey. A long sigh slipped though her lips. What *she* wanted was a career as a journalist. She had a double ma-jor in Software Engineering and Journal-ism. After graduating a year ago, her father had been furious when she declined to work for him, then applied for and accepted a job working for a small town newspaper away from home. Her father had said his only hope was for her to get married. That way her husband could not only give him a grandchild, but eventually take over the business, too. Lucky her.

How many times had her father set her up on a date? Too many to count. Boring duds whose personalities were as automated as a computer. She had to get away from the pressure, so she headed down the interstate in western Washington and didn't stop until she found a small town that needed a reporter. Since then her parents had only been down once to see her studio apartment, but they called her every day.

Stacey turned back to the front section and found her latest article about the California developer in town, Randolph Owens. He had purchased two thousand acres of land in the area, and her article focused on the impact such development could have on the land.

The wooden chair creaked as she leaned back, tapped the pencil against her lip and thought about old Randolph. He had refused to see her several times and wouldn't discuss his plans with her on the phone. She had seen a picture of the old guy in *Business World.* As usual he was smoking a big cigar, balding, heavyset, and, of course, tan. The first time she tried to meet with him at his office to get a quote from him, security had thrown her off the premises. Ever since then she hadn't written a kind word about him, hoping to anger him enough to flush him out. He had to be hiding something. Why else would he need security guards? Whatever it was, she would get to the bottom of it.

Stacey remained at her desk most of the day, making phone calls and reading up on the town's history for a future article. As she cleaned her desk, her mind was half on work and half on her ad. The paper had gone out early this morning, and still there was no response. As the day ended she began to panic. What would she do if no one answered the ad? She stared at the phone and wondered if she should pick it up right now and tell her parents the truth. After all, how angry could they get?

Instead of reaching for the phone on her desk, she reached for her purse and decided to call it a day.

"Nice article," Kyle Drew, the editor of the newspaper, said, coming up behind her. "If that doesn't piss the son-of-a-gun off, nothing will."

Stacey smiled at her boss. Praise from Kyle didn't come often, so when it did, she knew she'd done a good job. "Thanks." She stood and slipped on the navy blazer that complemented her dark blue slacks and contrasted with her white silk blouse. She kicked off her high heels and put on her sneakers.

"Pretty soon you'll be working for *The Seattle Times*," Kyle said.

"Maybe someday," Stacey said. She'd had an offer to work for *The Seattle Times*, but turned it down because she knew her father had arranged the opportunity. She had appreciated his efforts, but once, just once, she wanted to do something on her own. Independence was important to her, and she never took it for granted.

"Well, I'll see you tomorrow." Grabbing her purse and high heels, she headed for the door, the floor boards creaking with each step she took.

"Hey, Stacey," Kyle said. "Did you see this ad? 'Wanted: Temporary husband.' " His belly laugh rang in her ears. "Is that hilarious or what? Boy, that woman must be desperate." Suddenly Wanda Kellerman—a short, slim woman in her mid-fifties with a long narrow nose, frosted blond hair, and ruby lipstick—burst into the room, almost knocking Stacey down. She rushed everywhere, as if hurrying to get the story of the year. Wanda, the newspaper's advice columnist, eavesdropped on everyone's conversations, then inserted her own uninvited opinion. In the months Stacey had been with the newspaper the woman had yet to get her facts straight.

"I should get the scoop on that woman," Wanda said. "Wouldn't *that* be an interesting story?"

Stacey forced a smile. "Yeah. Interesting. Good night." She walked out of the old brick building and onto the sidewalk, thankful it wasn't raining, and wished she'd brought her overcoat as the wind picked up. Today even the quaint boutiques and smell of Emily's Bakery couldn't cheer her up. A chill ran over her body and she pulled her lapels more tightly together. The sky reflected her mood—dismal and gray.

Three days went by, and still no response to her ad. Stacey decided to wait one more day. Then, if nobody answered, she would call her parents and tell them the truth.

What a dumb idea, placing an ad in the local newspaper for a man! Her sister Faith had advised her. How crazy could she be, taking advice about finding a husband from a nun? People did desperate things during desperate times. No—people did stupid things during desperate times, and she could vouch for that.

As she entered the small office, the acrid smell of newspaper ink assailed her nostrils. She scanned the messy desks of the other three reporters, and felt proud she kept her area clean and tidy. After she put her purse in the drawer and her coat on the rack, she sifted through the mail. Her hands froze. She stared at the envelope addressed to *Temporary Husband*, hardly able to believe her eyes. Her pulse quickened.

She quickly read the brief letter. The man, who identified himself only as Aaron, said he was interested in the job and wanted to meet her at a local diner. Lady luck appeared to be on her side today.

Folding the letter, she stuffed it into her purse and sorted through the mail. Another reply. Wasting no time, she set up both appointments, two hours apart, then went to work on a new article. She had a hard time concentrating, and she had to admit, what she wrote about the fire in Harvey Hamilton's barn wasn't her best.

Finally lunchtime arrived. She entered

the little diner two blocks away from the office and surveyed the patrons. The smell of strong coffee and hot oil filled the air. Only one person was there—a male. His back was to her. She approached the table with caution, her stomach knotted, her palms clammy. As she reached the table and faced him, her hopes plummeted.

Staring back at her was a boy, probably not even out of high school yet, with straight, sandy brown hair, dimples, and acne on his forehead.

"Are you Aaron?"

He grinned. "Sure am."

Great. She forced a smile and shook her head. "I'm looking for a man older than I am, not a fifteen-year-old."

"I'm seventeen," he said defensively.

"And I'm twenty-six." She drew in a sharp breath and exhaled in a rush. "Thanks for responding, but this won't work." She returned to the office and waited to meet her next applicant, but he turned out to be worse—he was seventy-five years old. First she got a man too young, and the next was too old. She needed a husband, not a grand-father.

As Stacey walked back to her office she

wondered if she was being too picky. After all, the man just had to play a part; she wasn't really going to *marry* him. But, her father wouldn't buy it for a minute if she married a man nearly fifty years her senior.

As she walked to her desk, Kyle waved her inside. Sitting in his office behind a large messy desk, the editor was wide-eyed with excitement; his bushy brows nearly touched his hairline. "You'll never guess who just called." Without giving her time to respond, he said, "Randolph Owens. He's granted you an interview."

Stacey's lips parted, then curved into a triumphant smile. "Looks like I got to him."

"Sure does. So hustle over there right now."

"Now?"

"He said it's now or never."

She rolled her eyes skyward. "He wants everything done on his time, his terms, and his turf."

"What does it matter? You got the interview. Get going before he changes his mind." Kyle waved his hands as if shooing away a pesky fly.

Part of her wanted to take her time and

make the great and mighty Randolph Owens wait, but another part of her preferred to get the interview before he changed his mind. Stacey hurried out to her car. She drove down the main street of South Sound until the buildings turned from commercial to residential. Following a winding road that bordered a golf course, she reached a faded yellow building that looked more like a large shop than a business office. She parked diagonally in a horizontal parking slot, and paused when she reached the front door.

Both nervous and excited, she snatched her notepad from her purse, and entered the building. A dark room and empty receptionist's desk greeted her. At least there were no security guards this time.

She glanced around at the faded orange couch, green shag carpet, and brown curtains. A musty odor filled the room. The office hardly reflected the successful developer she had researched.

Dead silence hung in the room. She could hear herself breathing—a bit too quickly for her liking.

"Mr. Owens, are you here?"

She wondered if he was asleep behind

the closed office door. Her gaze dropped to the gap at the base of the door: no light seeped out from underneath. Maybe he stood her up, got her hopes up only to be dashed. Was he playing games with her in retaliation for her articles about him?

She really couldn't blame him if he was paying her back. Her articles had been unfair. She stepped closer to his office and knocked.

"Mr. Owens, it's Stacey Williams from *The South Sound Daily*. Are you here?"

Still no answer. She opened the door and peered inside. Randolph Owens was working away at his computer, his back to her. His large frame filled the chair, his broad shoulders stretching the material of his white shirt. From behind, Stacey couldn't detect a trace of gray hair, only thick black curls clipped short. Undoubtedly he used dye. She peered over his shoulder to look at his hands as they flew over the computer keyboard. Tan, large, and no wrinkles.

She cleared her throat to gain his attention, but when that didn't work she said, "Mr. Owens, I'm Stacey Williams from the newspaper. You called my boss and told him you were ready for an interview."

Randolph Owens held his hand up for her to wait, punched a few more keys, then whirled around in his chair and smiled.

Stacey held her breath, quickly scanned the nameplate on his desk, then glanced back at him. Randolph Owens was not the old man she had seen in photographs. Instead he was handsome, with incredibly deep blue eyes—what was that color called? Cobalt blue? He had a healthy-looking tan, which accentuated the whiteness of his straight teeth. His aristocratic nose was in perfect proportion to his face—not too large, not too small.

The man could have jumped out of a magazine.

Questions spun in her mind, but none of them was about why he was here and what he intended to build in the South Sound area.

"You're Randolph Owens?" Stacey asked, narrowing her stare at him.

"The one and only." He held his arms out to the side in a take it or leave it manner.

Her gaze dropped to his athletic build. She tried to ignore the stirring in her stomach at the mere sight of him.

"I expected someone whose pen runs all over the pages to be more talkative," he said.

She darted her gaze back to his face, slightly embarrassed, and flipped open her notepad. "I, uh, expected someone older."

The chair squeaked when he shifted, and he folded his arms over his broad chest. "Why is that?"

She clicked her pen open, ready to write. "My research depicted you as being older. And you've developed so many areas, I just thought . . ." She set the tip of her pen on the paper, ready to take notes. As she gazed over at him, fascinated by the sleek slant of his jaw, his perfectly shaped lips, and thick dark brows, her heart beat a little faster.

Stacey chastised herself for reacting to him. When had a man ever affected her this way? Never. And she wanted to make sure it stayed that way, especially where Randolph Owens was concerned.

"Land development is my father's interest." He gestured for her to sit down in the nearest chair. "I'm named after him, but normally I go by my middle name, Lance."

"I would have appreciated your receptionist telling me that when I called." Now all those hours of research were wasted. Although many times the acorn didn't fall far from the tree. "So you're saying that you aren't here to develop the area?"

He held a finger up. "I never said that. Don't misquote me again."

"I never quoted you," Stacey said.

"Yes, that's right. Instead you made a lot of assumptions at my expense." The smile faded from his face, and his eyes took on an angry gleam.

"You wouldn't take my calls, or return them. You wouldn't grant me an interview, and you had me manhandled by your security and thrown off your property."

"You weren't invited."

"Well, now I am. So tell me, why are you here? And why do you need security in a small rural town?"

"I thought you already figured that out," Lance said.

Her hand tightened on the pen. The man wouldn't give her a straight answer. He was hiding something. What could it be? "You'd make a wonderful politician, Mr. Owens. You've mastered the art of saying nothing when answering a question."

"Have I?"

He tried to sound innocent, but Stacey wasn't fooled. "Okay, let's stop playing games. What kind of business do you run? And why here?"

He lifted his shoulders. "I needed a change of pace."

Stacey drew in a deep breath, trying her best to remain calm. "You've bought a large amount of land. Are you saying you have no intention of building here, or starting a new development? Or do you intend to try your hand at farming?"

"I might." He smiled again, but the hard set of his eyes told her he was anything but happy. "You've certainly done your homework. I'm surprised a small town would have such an aggressive reporter."

"Assertive."

"What?"

"I prefer to be called assertive, not aggressive. And you're changing the subject." Stacey tapped the top of the pen against her bottom lip.

"Am I?"

She set her pen back on the notepad, and noticed that his stare dropped to her lips before returning to her eyes. "Why did you ask me to come here? Obviously it wasn't for an interview."

For a moment Lance studied her. "You're not at all what I expected."

"What do you mean?"

"I didn't think such a beautiful woman could be so vicious with a pen. I just wanted to meet the person who's trying so hard to delve into my private matters."

She held his stare. "What business did you say you were in?"

"Why are you so interested in what I'm doing?"

"It's news."

Lance shook his head. "I think there's more to it."

She squeezed her lips together. He'd hit it right on the head. She was investigating a chemical plant, located on the outskirts of town, that she suspected of dumping hazardous waste. The only problem was, she couldn't prove it. Lance Owens had to be connected, which would explain his tight security and buying the land. "Sorry. You're way off," she said.

He raised his brows, obviously unconvinced. "If there's anything else I can do for you, just let me know," he said. His chair screeched as he pushed out of it. Reluctantly, she stood and made her way to the door. He followed her. "Oh, by the way, did anyone respond to the 'Husband Wanted' ad?"

"Why? Interested?" She inhaled a whiff of his cologne. Musk—her favorite.

He drew his brows together. "Maybe. Or maybe I'm just curious."

"Curious about what?" Stacey reached for the door handle.

"Curious about why your office number's on that ad."

Heat surged to her face. Darn. Why couldn't she control her reaction? "I'm in charge of the ads."

"Then why isn't your number on all the ads in the paper?"

"We share that duty in the office."

"Really?"

"Yes, really." She couldn't even convince herself. "Besides, why would I need to advertise for a husband?"

"You tell me."

Her lips curved up, but as hard as she tried, she couldn't form a believable smile. "You sure have an active imagination."

"Not as good as yours, judging by your articles."

She glared at him. "Good day, Mr. Owens."

He dipped his head, his confident grin never wavering.

Lance sat in a quiet restaurant at a table for two on the outskirts of town. He hoped his sources had been right about Stacey's frequenting this restaurant for dinner. After she had left, he'd spent the next hour researching *her*. Stacey Williams, daughter of computer mogul Stan Williams, had supposedly recently eloped. Funny how she wasn't wearing a wedding ring when she came to his office earlier today. Now he was more convinced than ever that she had put the ad for a temporary husband in the newspaper.

And he intended to get the job.

Twenty minutes later Stacey entered the restaurant, and was seated at the table next to him. He'd arranged it that way. Lance glanced over at her and nodded a hello. "So we meet again."

She opened her menu and stared at it. "I guess that'll happen in a small town."

"Have you found a husband yet?"

"No." She looked at him, her error evident in her reddening face. "I mean, the person who placed the ad hasn't found anyone yet."

"I know someone interested in the job."

"Oh?" She tried to sound uninterested, but one glimpse at her hands squeezing the menu told him different. "Who's that?"

"Me." He waited until she looked at him. "May I join you?"

"I prefer to eat alone."

"Do you also prefer to let the entire town know you're the one who placed the ad?"

Stacey lifted her hands, palms up, gesturing to the seat across from her. "Be my guest."

Lance settled into the chair and leaned forward, his elbows resting on the table. "I think we can help each other."

"I can't imagine how." She returned her attention to the menu, gazing at it as if she were reading a good novel.

He scanned the pure lines of her face, the curves of her lips, and her long silky blond hair. Why she needed to hire a husband was beyond logic. When he had first glanced at her in his office she had taken his breath away. "Why don't you tell me why you need to advertise in the newspaper for a husband?"

"It's none of your business."

He forced a laugh. "That's a good one. Everything in my life is your business, but you won't explain an ad you placed to me."

She glared at him, then blurted out the truth. "I told my parents I was married, and they're having a reception for my husband and me this weekend."

He rubbed his jaw. "Why'd you do that?"

She hesitated. "Because my father's been pressuring me to get married and"— she looked him straight in the eyes— "I just wanted him off my back."

"And you think lying to him will make the problem go away?"

"Yes. No. I don't know. It sounded good at the time." She dropped the menu on the table and clasped her hands in her lap.

"Tell your parents the truth," Lance said.

"I've tried. But they've been so happy and excited since I told them I eloped." A moment of silence arose between them. "I didn't have the courage. Besides . . ." Her gaze dropped to her hands. "I thought I was helping them."

"How?"

She hesitated before meeting his eyes. "My father's not well. I wanted to cheer him up, give my parents good news for a change."

"I'm sure they'd understand."

She forced a breath out. "You don't know my father." As she narrowed her stare at him, worry lines formed on her forehead. "Why are you interested in the job?"

"Business."

"Are you going to elaborate on that? Or evade yet another one of my questions?"

Lance reminded himself of how much he needed Stacey's father, with all his business and financial contacts. Despite how much it pained him to even think about his past, he knew he had to tell her at least the shortened version.

"Well?" Her gaze never left his face.

"In California I had it all, a successful computer business, an intelligent business partner—who happened to be my best friend—and a beautiful fiancée. Then one day I came to work and found my partner and fiancée had run off together and taken my company with them."

Her lips parted, and for a moment she said nothing. Then she whispered, "I'm sorry."

He shrugged her sympathy off. "I'm better off without them. Took me months to come to that conclusion. So now I'm starting over."

"Why the security?"

"My partner took everything except for a new project we'd been working on. I had the only copy."

"And you think they'll come back and steal it?"

"Who knows?"

The waitress came to take their orders, and departed.

"I guess I don't understand how we could help each other," Stacey said.

Lance hesitated. "I know who your father is."

"And you want him to buy your product?"

"No. I just need a couple of contacts from him, that's all. In return I'll pose as your husband until it's the right time to tell him the truth." When she didn't respond, he added, "I'd say that's a pretty fair business deal."

"I want to make it clear that our arrangement remains strictly business, nothing more."

Lance smiled. "Agreed." He extended his hand. When her palm touched his, a heat ignited in the pit of his stomach. She definitely interested him, but he wasn't stupid enough to fall into a woman's trap again. Besides, getting his company up and running was his first priority. Nothing else would clog his mind—not even the beautiful Stacey Williams.

His life may have been in shambles for the last six months, but his luck seemed to be changing. Good fortune would bring him face to face with Stan Williams, a major player in the computer industry, founder and owner of Microland. Lance intended to capitalize on this meeting.

Stacey knew she didn't have a choice. Lance Owens was the perfect candidate. Successful. Handsome. Not too old, not too young. And not married. Her choice was either choosing Lance Owens or telling her father the truth. The truth might devastate her father, which wouldn't bode well with his health.

Throughout the rest of the dinner Stacey found herself enjoying Lance Owens' company. He was fascinating, intelligent, witty, and charming. Just the man her father would have picked for her. If she didn't know better, she might have guessed that her father sent Lance here to play the part of her husband, but then there was no way her father could have ever found out that she had lied to him . . . or could he?

Chapter Two

The house was just as Lance pictured it, large, lavish, contemporary beachfront home located on Orcas Island in the San Juan Islands. As he walked behind Stacey, suitcases in hand, up to the front door, he wondered if she would be able to pull off this charade. He knew he would get through it. In fact, he found himself liking the role he had to play. For some reason, he felt as comfortable with Stacey as if he had known her his whole life.

Caution crossed his mind the moment the thought did—he didn't need or want to get involved with someone right now.

Besides, Stacey had made it quite clear

that she didn't want to get married, possibly ever. She appeared to be a woman who liked to be in control of every situation in her life, yet she put herself in this compromising position. Why was it so hard for her to tell her parents the truth? Even though he had never met Stan Williams, Lance admired him. Microland was one of the largest computer software companies in the world, and always stayed one step ahead of even the toughest competition.

Someday, Lance would build his own business and turn his computer company into a major conglomerate like Microland. He looked forward to meeting the man who had started it all.

"Ready?" Stacey asked.

He nodded.

She took a deep breath, knocked on the door, and entered. They stepped into the foyer, which opened into a large living room with a vaulted ceiling, two ivory leather sofas, a matching recliner, and a white and gray marble fireplace lit with a warm fire. "We're here," Stacey said.

"Stacey," her mother cried, rushing across the room, spreading her arms wide, embracing her daughter.

Her father pushed out of his easy-chair and strolled across the hardwood floor to meet them. He kissed her on the cheek.

"We are so happy and excited about your marriage," Carol said.

Lance set the suitcases on the floor and soon all eyes were on him.

"Mom. Dad. This is Randolph Owens." Her smile wavered as she glanced at him. "He likes to be called by his middle name, Lance." She paused, then added, "Lance, this is my mother, Carol, and my father, Stan."

"Randolph?" Stan said, narrowing his stare at Stacey. "I thought you said his name was Rick."

"No, I said Randolph," Stacey said a little too quickly.

"It doesn't matter, Stan," Carol said. "He's our son-in-law now." She gave Lance a warm embrace. Carol reminded Lance of many of the executive wives he had met in California: not a blond hair out of place, slim build, and dressed in nice slacks and blouse despite being at a beach-house. Stan Williams was much shorter than Lance had judged by the pictures he had seen of him. Stan's thinning hair had turned pure white, and his face was pale.

Stan was next, giving him a hearty handshake. "Randolph Owens," he said, mulling the name over. "You're not related to Owens Technology, are you?"

"I own it," Lance said, surprised Stan had heard of his small company. After his business fiasco, the name of his company was about the only thing he was able to hold on to.

Stan slapped him on the back, a smile as wide as Puget Sound spreading on his face. "Come in, my boy." As they walked into the living room, Stan said, "Stacey, you couldn't have picked a better husband than if I'd picked him for you. This young man is going places."

Lance grinned at Stacey as he followed Stan and Carol into the living room.

Stacey rolled her eyes and made a face at him.

Gosh, she was beautiful. He almost wished . . .

"Now tell us how you two met," Carol said, anticipation in her voice. "I want to hear everything, all the little details."

"Let them sit down first," Stan said.

Lance followed Stacey over to one of the sofas and sat beside her. Carol perched on the edge of the sofa opposite them, her hands folded in her lap, her eyes wide with interest and excitement.

Lance couldn't help but notice how nervous Stacey looked. He slipped his hand over hers and gave her a reassuring squeeze. She glanced over at him and smiled. Not once did she try to remove her hand from his.

"We met while I was covering a story," Stacey said.

Stan rolled his eyes skyward. "That darned journalism career of hers. I guess it came in handy for one good thing. So you started dating right away?"

"Yes, sir," Lance said. "I took one look at Stacey and knew I wanted to live with her the rest of my life."

Stacey looked at him, her eyes wide. They hadn't rehearsed that part on the drive over, but it just felt right so Lance had to say it. He gazed over at Stan and Carol and could tell they bought the story. "So I spent every waking moment with Stacey." She gave him a warning glare, but he didn't stop. What could he say? He was on a roll.

"After a few weeks I knew I had to marry her. My business takes up so much of my time. I was afraid if I waited I would lose her to another man. I didn't want her to slip through my fingers. So I asked her to marry me and she said yes."

"Are you going to be moving to California, then?" Stan asked.

"Why would we move there?" Stacey asked.

Stan drew his thinning white brows together. "Owens Technology is in California. You'll have to live where your husband's business is."

"Actually, sir," Lance said, "I'm living in South Sound right now and looking to build a bigger company." For once Lance told the truth. He hated lying, especially to someone he respected so much.

"Oh, Stan," Carol said, "Isn't that wonderful? They'll be living in Washington where we can see them more often."

"You know, before you do that, maybe we could talk about future plans for both of our companies," Stan said. "After all, you'll be taking over my business someday, son."

Lance's heart beat faster. *Take over Mi-*

croland! Wouldn't that be a dream come true!

"Dad, don't you think you're moving things a little too quickly? We haven't been here more than five minutes and you're already merging companies." Stacey's moist hand squeezed on Lance's fingers.

"Never hurts to look ahead."

"Oh, Stan," Carol said, disgust in her voice.

He held up his hands in surrender. "Okay. I'll drop the subject for now." He pointed to Lance and said, "We can talk about it after breakfast tomorrow."

"Whatever you say, sir."

"Stop calling me 'sir'," Stan commanded. "Call me Dad. After all, that's who I am to you now."

Lance smiled. He liked Stan Williams. And he could tell he had won Stan's approval too. Lance wondered how he would react when he learned that their marriage wasn't real. Guilt twisted his gut. He hated deception—it reminded him of his ex-fiancée's betrayal. And now here he was lying to one of the most respected men in software development, a leader in the field, a man Lance had admired for years and tried to emulate while building his own business.

Lance listened to the conversation as it turned to the party, the guest list, and news of family members. Each time he glanced at Stacey he felt a tightening in his chest. From the moment he met her he had noticed too much about her, like the way her eyes turned a dark shade of green when suspicion entered her mind, the way she tilted her head in thought, and the way she tipped her chin up when she wanted her way and couldn't get it. Independence. She had plenty of that, yet she carried a certain vulnerability. He liked the combination, and was surprised that she brought out the primal urge in him to protect her.

He grinned at the thought.

Fisting his free hand, he resisted the need to reach out and stroke her hair. Was it silky? Would it glide between his fingers if he grabbed thick mounds of it in his hands?

After an hour passed, Stan stood. "I'll go light up the barbeque. How do you like your steak, Lance?"

"Medium rare."

A hearty chuckle bubbled from Stan.

"Just how I like mine. Son, I think we're going to get along just fine."

"I'd like that," Lance said.

"Our housekeeper is sick with the flu, so I'm cooking tonight," Carol said. "Make yourselves comfortable."

Stacey's body hadn't stopped shaking since she had arrived, and it wasn't from the cold, rainy weather, either. How would she be able to pull this off? What about Lance? A weekend was a long time. Suddenly she wished she had never thought of this stupid plan. She must have been temporarily crazy at the time. Right now, she was outright insane to go through with it.

Stacey stood and wandered the room, stopping at the window to glance out at the water, her arms folded over her chest. She listened to the fire crackle in the fireplace, the flames casting a glow on the nearby walls.

Lance seemed perfectly content to be the one in charge, which worried her. First he insisted on taking his car, and now he was making up his own story. She had to be in control of this situation if she was ever going to get through it. So far he had cooperated, but she hardly knew him.

The ache in her stomach hadn't subsided. In fact, the longer they were here at the beach house the worse it became. She could still hear the ring of happiness in her parents' voices when they told her about the party they had planned. All their closest family and friends were coming to celebrate. Her parents had even asked for a picture of her and her new husband so they could send it in to the newspaper.

Stacey swallowed. At the time, she had told them the honest truth: no picture existed. Oh, dear. She had dug herself into a grave-sized hole this time.

Her thoughts turned to Lance. She couldn't believe her luck when he had volunteered for the job. He was the perfect candidate.

Too perfect. Her mind flowed with suspicion. Could her father have set her up? No. Impossible. There was no way he could have found out she had lied. She hadn't given him enough details about the elopement, or about her new husband.

Lance came up from behind her and rested his hands on her shoulders. She could feel his warm breath brush her cheek, and smell the rich scent of his cologne, an essence that made her knees go weak.

"I'm practicing my part," he said, amusement in his voice.

Everything between them was a lie. She had to remember that. With Lance's good looks and charm she could easily fall under his spell. She moved over to the stereo system, out of his reach, trying her best to ignore the tingling sensation his touch evoked.

Music would be nice and relaxing. Just what she needed. She reached out and touched the power button. The radio turned on, and as she attempted to shut it off she accidentally pressed the volume. The noise reached an ear-piercing level. She tried another button to shut the radio off and the CD player opened.

Suddenly beside her, Lance pushed her hand aside, turned down the volume, and closed the CD. "I can see you're mechanically inclined," he said, followed by a chuckle.

"Very funny." Stacey gave him a sharp glare as she walked passed him and stared at a painting on the wall. Now was not the time to tell him she was an engineer.

"You need to relax, Stacey," Lance said.

"I *would* be relaxed if we had taken my car."

He gave her a puzzled look as if he didn't follow.

"Driving relaxes me."

"Your car wouldn't start."

"That's because you were too impatient. If you would have waited five minutes I would have gotten it started."

"Five minutes?"

"Once it starts it purrs like a content kitty."

"I prefer to drive. And my car starts with the first turn of the key."

A heavy silence filled the space between them. Neither one spoke for several minutes.

"We need to stick to our plan," Stacey said, her voice not more than a whisper.

"*Our* plan? You mean *your* plan."

"I hired you to be part of a team. I expect you to hold your end up." She folded her arms over her chest.

"Or what, you'll fire me?" Lance laughed.

Over her shoulder she narrowed a glare at him.

In three strides he stood before her, and rubbed the side of her arms. "Don't worry. Your secret's safe with me."

"That's hardly reassuring."

The smile that played on his lips teased and taunted her.

"Dinner's ready," Carol said, setting a steaming bowl on the table.

Stacey led the way into the dining room and settled in her usual spot in the middle of the table. Lance sat across from her, and her mother and father sat at each end.

"Help yourself to everything, Lance. We're not formal," Carol said.

"So, make up any good stories lately?" Stan asked, laughing at his joke as he handed Stacey a bowl of mashed potatoes.

Did he know? Was he talking about her fictitious marriage or something else? She couldn't tell. With as much ease as possible she said, "I only write the truth."

Lance forced a bitter laugh. "That's a good one."

Stacey's eyes narrowed as she glared at him.

"I can see you feel the same way about her being a reporter as I do," Stan said.

"You don't know the half of it." He smiled at her.

Stan nodded, then bit into a piece of steak.

"Stacey, you never did tell us where you got married," Carol said.

"In a chapel," Stacey said at the same time Lance said, "In Vegas."

"In a chapel in Las Vegas," Stacey quickly added. A moment of heavy tension filled the room. She waited for the final boom to hit, the announcement that her parents knew she was trying to deceive them. She held her breath.

"I must say I was disappointed that you ran off to get married," Stan said. His stare seemed to burn a hole right though Stacey's head.

She glanced at her filled plate.

"I'm afraid that was my idea, sir, and I apologize for that. Stacey wanted to have a large wedding in a church, but I insisted we marry right away."

Stacey looked over at her father and watched his expression change into an easy, forgiving smile. She got the reprimanding glare and Lance got understanding! How fair was that? Men!

Lance had her parents eating out of his hand. They welcomed him with open arms, listened to his every word, and understood his motives even if they didn't agree with them. She knew she should be thankful for their reaction—instead it irritated her like a bad rash.

"Did you have anyone stand up for you?" Carol asked.

"A woman," Stacey said as Lance said, "A man." They looked at each other.

"They provide things like that at those places," Stan said with a wave of his hand.

Her mother persisted with her questions. "What did you wear?"

"A white dress."

"Oh, I wish I could have seen you. Was the dress short or long?"

Stacey hesitated. "Short."

"Was your family there, Lance?" Carol asked.

"No," he said, shaking his head. "In fact, they still don't know I'm married."

Carol frowned. "Why's that?"

Stacey cleared her throat, hoping to gain Lance's attention and give him the signal to shut up, but he wouldn't look at her. She knew he was just being difficult.

"Everyone in my family has a busy career. Most of the time I don't even know where they are."

A sympathetic expression crossed Carol's face.

Stacey decided changing the subject would be best. Talking about their imaginary wedding would only get them deeper into trouble. She had no idea if she would be able to recall these details later. "When will Faith and Pamela be here?"

The conversation changed and remained that way throughout the rest of dinner. Afterwards Stacey helped her mother with the dishes while Stan and Lance retired into the entertainment room, the only room in the house in which Stacey's mother allowed Stan to smoke cigars. An hour went by before they met back in the living room.

"It's been a long day. Maybe we should call it a night," Lance said as he slid his arm around Stacey.

"You must be tired," Carol said, her brows creasing together and wrinkling her forehead in concern.

Lance picked up the suitcases and trailed behind Stacey and her mother up the stairs. Carol entered the bedroom first, flicking the light on. The large room was decorated in rich dark green and gold. A dark wood dresser filled one wall, matching the nightstands and headboard. The connected bathroom was adorned in the same regal colors and pattern. The room looked elegant, fit for royalty.

"I decorated it myself," Carol said. "I even had a new king-size bed brought in just for the newlyweds." She turned and smiled at them, a gleam in her eyes. She kissed her daughter on the cheek, then gently gripped Lance's arm. "We are so happy you're part of our family now. You have no idea how wonderful this news is for Stacey's father and me." She walked to the door and turned, a grin playing at the corners of her mouth. "Sweet dreams." She raised her eyebrows in a teasing manner before she shut the door.

After her footsteps disappeared down the stairs Stacey raised her hands in the air, then let them smack her sides. "Great. I forgot about our sleeping arrangements." She heaved a deep sigh.

"Why don't we just share the bed?" Lance said, as if the solution was obvious.

She frowned.

He forced a breath out. "I won't touch you. Promise." Lance hesitated, then shook his head. "Stacey, I don't think I can continue to play this game."

The blood drained from her face. "What do you mean? We had an agreement. I hired you to act."

"I'm not an actor, and I don't like lying to your parents. They're nice people."

"Please don't do this. It's only for one weekend, that's all. I'll pay you double, triple—whatever you want, but don't tell my parents the truth. Not now." She rubbed her temples, then paced to the other side of the room, pivoted, and faced him.

"Stacey," he said, a warning in his tone, "you've got to tell them sometime. I think the sooner the better."

Her hand shook as she held it up, palm outward, to stop him from continuing his line of reasoning. "I'll tell them in my own time. I . . . I just can't tell them right now."

"Why? Why are you so afraid of them?"

"I'm not afraid of them," she said. "I just don't want to hurt them. My grandmother died two months ago and now with my father finding out he has cancer . . ." She clasped her hands together. "Don't you see why I did this? My parents, my family need something good to happen in their lives. They need good news. Our marriage has done that." She could see doubt in his eyes.

"But we aren't married," he reminded her.

"I know." She plopped her suitcase on the bed. "Can we talk about this tomorrow?" When Lance didn't reply, she looked over at him. He was unbuttoning his shirt. Stacey quickly shifted her gaze, opened her suitcase, grabbed her toiletry bag and clothes, then hurried into the bathroom.

Stacey took her time, hoping Lance would be asleep in bed by the time she finished. But when she stepped out Lance sat on the bed, in his pajamas.

"Do you always sleep in your sweats?" Lance asked.

"I get cold."

"I'll keep you warm," Lance said with humor in his voice. "Isn't that what a husband is for?"

Stacey climbed in bed, lined pillows down the center, puffed her pillow, turned on her side and closed her eyes. She stiffened when the bed dipped and he slipped in between the sheets on the other side.

"Are the pillows really necessary?" When she didn't answer he said, "Heck, if I was going to attack you, I would have done it in the car, not in your parents' home under their noses."

She remained silent.

"Fine. Have it your way." He turned on his side, opposite her, punched his pillow, and flopped his head down. A deep sigh followed. "Goodnight, darling."

Inwardly, Stacey had to laugh at his sarcasm. Her plan would work just fine—they already sounded like a married couple having their first fight.

Chapter Three

Whu hen Stacey woke the next morning
she found the other half of the bed empty.
Good. She glanced at the clock—10:00.
She hadn't fallen asleep until the early
morning hours, especially since Lance had
hogged all the covers. Once in the night she
woke up to find herself snuggled up against
him; the pillows that had divided the bed
had been kicked onto the floor. He was
warm, though. She never knew that sharing
a bed with a man could feel so comforting,
so right.

She sighed and closed her eyes. That's
not how she wanted to feel, not toward this
man. Lack of sleep must be playing with

her emotions. She hadn't had a good night's sleep since she'd invented this absurd story.

After showering and changing into blue jeans, a sweater, and sneakers, she ambled downstairs. As she passed the glass doors of her father's office she spotted Lance sitting across from him. They appeared to be deep in discussion about something. Were they talking about Lance taking over her father's company? Surely Lance would refuse . . . or would he?

Her knees felt suddenly weak, her mouth dry. She knew nothing about Lance. Would the temptation be too great for him? She should have dug up information on father and son. Her sloppy research could prove detrimental to her. At least her father had heard of Lance's company, but that told her nothing about his character.

Wandering into the kitchen, she found her mother sitting at the breakfast table, a pad and pencil in front of her.

"Good morning," Stacey said.

Her mother smiled, only glancing at her briefly.

Opening the refrigerator, Stacey pulled out a pitcher of orange juice and poured herself a large glass. "Mom?" She had to wait several seconds before her mother looked up. "What's Dad talking to Lance about?"

Carol shrugged. "Probably business. He's so excited to have a son-in-law he can talk computer lingo with. You should have heard him last night, going on and on about Lance. He's happy as a clam." Her mother's wide smile slowly faded as she studied Stacey.

"What's wrong?" Stacey asked, sitting down across from her mother.

"Oh, I wasn't going to say anything, but it worries me that you two married so soon after meeting one another. I hope you can make the marriage work."

"Don't worry, Mom. Everything will work out just fine."

Carol reached out and covered Stacey's hand. "I only want you to be happy. Since you've arrived you seem nervous, not your usual self. You're afraid you've made a mistake, aren't you? You think you rushed into this marriage, and now you're having second thoughts."

Here was her chance to tell the truth. "Mom." She dragged in a shaky breath and exhaled, but that didn't dull the painful lump in her throat. She loved her mother, and the thought of hurting her tore Stacey up inside.

"Marriage is difficult," Carol said. "It doesn't get any easier. Give it time. I can see by the way Lance looks at you he loves you." She patted her daughter's hand before she picked up the pencil and tapped it on the paper. "Just don't do anything impulsive like a quick divorce. I think that would just about kill your father. You know how he feels about divorce, no matter what the circumstances are."

Oh, great. How did that minor detail slip her mind? Her father must have lectured her a million times on marriage. This situation just seemed to grow worse by the minute. "Mom, I'm going for a walk on the beach."

"You always do that when you have things to work out." Carol gave her an understanding smile.

As Stacey rose from the chair, her mother stared at the paper and said, "Your father keeps delaying his operation."

Stunned, Stacey could only stare at her

mother. She opened her mouth to say something, but she couldn't find her voice.

"The doctor said he's confident he'll be able to get it all, if he operates soon." Carol expelled a sigh of frustration. "Your father thinks he's invincible."

Stacey met her mother's soft blue eyes, her concern so clear in them. "I'll do whatever I can to help."

The muscles relaxed in her mother's face, softening the wrinkles. "You already have."

Stacey frowned in question.

Her mother continued. "Knowing you've married such a fine man, and that the Williams name will be carried on has brought such a sense of peace to your father's life—and to mine. You've made us so proud and happy. I'm sure now he'll schedule the operation soon."

Stacey forced a smile. "I think I'm going to take that walk now." She snatched a coat off a hook by the back door and stepped out onto the deck. She strode past the heated swimming pool and the hot tub, both steaming warm vapors into the chilled air, then quickly dissipating. She skipped down the stairs and strolled along the rocky beach. She thought more clearly out in the fresh air, the salty smell of the water always a comfort. A cool breeze blew strands of hair in her face. The sun broke out and patches of brilliant blue contrasted with the bleached white of puffy cumulus clouds.

She glanced down at the ground and turned over an empty clam shell with the toe of her shoe. Normally she would walk up and down the shore until she had worked her problems out. And without a doubt, she always came up with a good solution. Today, she could walk around the island fifty times and still have no answers, no excuses—because there were none.

"Stacey," Lance called out from the deck of the house. The rich timbre of his voice was becoming familiar and oddly comforting.

He jogged down to her, looking rugged in jeans and a sweat shirt, his hair disheveled from the breeze. "Would you like company?"

She shrugged.

He slipped his arm around her shoulders, and when she gave him a questioning glance he said, "Your father's watching us from the window." They strolled at a slow pace.

"What did you two talk about?" She asked, even though she knew the answer.

"Business."

"So, did he draw up papers to make you CEO of his company?" Even though her tone was sarcastic she was serious. She knew her father never waited on anything.

"I told him I wasn't interested."

"That won't stop him."

"I know." He glanced at her, stopped, and turned her into his arms. "I was hoping to put him off for a day or two." His eyes flickered to her lips before his head lowered, his kiss brief and gentle.

"Is my father still watching us?"

He glanced at the house, then back to her. "No. I just wondered what it would be like to kiss you. I've wondered that all night long." He bent his head again. This time he kissed her slowly. His hands glided inside her coat and rested on her waist, their warmth seeping through the material to her skin.

His kiss, his touch shouldn't feel this good. A giddy sensation surfaced in her stomach, followed by a twinge of disappointment when he lifted his head.

He dragged in a deep breath and exhaled slowly while he studied her reaction. "That was nice," he said in a husky voice.

"Yes, it was." But she didn't want it to be so nice. She didn't want to look forward to his kisses, or the next time she would see him, or be with him. She had only known Lance a few days and already felt drawn to him.

She resumed walking. When he didn't follow she glanced over her shoulder. For a moment he remained where he was, as if anchored to the beach, staring at her. Seconds later he caught up, draped his arm around her shoulders, and strolled with her.

Was she starting to believe in this fantasy she had created? No—none of this was real. She had to remember that. Lance was merely playing a part, but, darn, he was playing it well. He even had her believing he was in love with her. And what about her feelings? She was definitely physically attracted to him, but nothing more. Yeah, that was it, just attracted to him physically. Whew. What a relief. Falling in love with Lance was a complication she didn't need.

* * *

Lance really enjoyed their walk. They talked about their childhoods, college days, politics, subjects they liked and disliked, and what they hoped to accomplish in the future. Lance had never talked with his ex-fiancée, Sylvia, this much or about this many subjects during the five years they had dated.

As they climbed the long set of stairs to the deck, Lance noticed several people congregated in the kitchen. One heavyset woman wore a short blue habit with a matching blue dress.

"My sisters are here," Stacey said, and smiled.

Lance followed her into the house, and watched the women exchange hugs. Soon their gazes turned to him. He smiled and extended his hand while Stacey gave the introductions. "Lance, this is my older sister, Faith. And this is my younger sister, Pamela."

"He's so handsome," Faith said, raised her brows several times, then giggled.

Lance couldn't hide his surprise.

"I might be a nun, but I'm still a woman.

I can admire a handsome man, can't I?" All three sisters laughed.

Sister Faith wasn't like any nun he'd ever met, not that he had met very many in his lifetime. "I'm not sure what I should call you, Sister, Sister Faith—"

"How about Faith? I'm your sister-in-law now." Taking a step forward, she gave him a hearty hug. "My, he's a hunk!"

Heat rushed up Lance's neck and into his face. Faith definitely was unlike any nun he had ever met! He shot a glance at the swinging kitchen door which seemed so close, yet so far away.

Stacey laughed. "Faith, you're embarrassing him. I think that's the first time I've seen him blush."

Lance ran his finger inside his collar and cleared his throat. "I think I'll find a more neutral territory, like your father's office."

"Not so fast," Pamela said, bumping her sister aside with her slim hip. "My turn." She spread her arms wide.

This was the friendliest family Lance had ever met. Everyone showered him with hugs and kisses from the time he had walked through the door. That is, everyone but Stacey, the one woman he wanted hugs and kisses from, the woman who was supposed to be his wife. He embraced Pamela. As soon as she released her hold, he exited the room like a rabbit slipping from a mountain lion's claws.

He could hear the three women's laughter clear into the living room. His gaze dropped to Stan, seated in his chair reading the newspaper. "Don't let them bother you. When they get together they're a bunch of teases. But now that you're in the family, we're evening the score."

"Evening the score?"

"You know, the number of men to women. And after you have a few sons we'll finally have a voice in this family."

Lance smiled. He suspected Stan *was* the voice in the family and always had the final word. Lance had been raised in a balanced family. His mother and father, both successful in business, treated each other as equals, and he'd grown up with only one sister, no brothers. They all got along pretty well, but they were so involved in their careers they rarely saw or spoke to one another. Being part of the Williams family felt good, and made him long to be part of a family unit, part of a whole that came together and supported one another. Ironically, he fit into this family, almost as if he was the missing piece of the puzzle.

The doorbell rang and Stacey fired a questioning glance at her sisters, both wearing sly grins. "What's going on? Who's at the door?"

"Surprise," Faith sang out.

"We're throwing you a surprise bridal shower, a belated one," Pamela said. "Unfortunately, Mom wouldn't let us have a male stripper."

"Real classy, Pam." Stacey led the way into the living room just as her mother opened the door. A group of women, friends and relatives, congregated in the foyer, chatting and laughing.

"Looks like it's time for us to leave, Lance," Stan said, making a quick departure.

Carol grabbed Lance by the arm before he could retreat with Stan into the entertainment room. "Ladies, this is my new son-in-law, Lance Owens."

He nodded his hello to the group before he met Stacey's stare. He stepped over to her, gave her a quick kiss on the lips, and said, "Have fun, honey." He produced one of his charming smiles, then hustled away, shutting the door behind him.

Honey? Where'd that come from? Stacey couldn't have asked for a better actor than if she had hired Sean Connery.

"Stacey," her younger cousin said, "he's a real catch. I can't believe you found him in that dinky little town you live in. What is it called—South something?"

"South Sound."

"Maybe I should visit South Sound," another said.

And yet another added, "Does he have a brother?"

Stacey hesitated. She didn't know. She had never asked him. Thinking quickly and hoping she was right, she said, "Sorry. No brother." Groans could be heard from many of the ladies. While the group entered the living room and sat down, Stacey pulled Faith aside. "Why didn't you tell me about this?"

"I didn't have time."

"We have to talk."

"Can't it wait?"

"Stacey, Faith, what are you two doing over there?" Carol called. "Come join us."

"We were, uh, going into the kitchen to get the refreshments." Before her mother could respond Stacey hustled Faith into the kitchen.

"What's so urgent?"

"I took your advice."

Wrinkles formed on Faith's forehead as her dark brown eyes narrowed. "What are you talking about?"

"I put an ad in the paper for a temporary husband."

The blood seeped from Faith's face, making her appear white as snow. "I was kidding when I suggested that!"

"Shh!" Stacey said. "How was I supposed to know that?"

Faith lowered her voice to a whisper. "Are you telling me you're not really married to this guy? You hired him?"

Stacey nodded while wearing a sheepish expression.

"Of all the stupid things to do!"

"It was *your* idea." Stacey placed her hands on her hips.

Carol burst into the kitchen. "What is holding you girls up in here? Stacey, you're being very rude to your guests." She whipped open the refrigerator and grabbed a couple of trays, and carried them out.

Wanting to get away from her sister's glare, Stacey picked up a bowl sitting on the counter.

"You're going to have to tell Mom and Dad before tonight," Faith said.

"I can't." Stacey slipped out into the living room and placed the food on the table, then joined the group. She leaned over and whispered in her mother's ear, "Thanks for giving me time to clean up and change."

"You and Lance were gone so long on your walk, there wasn't time," Carol said.

Throughout the party Stacey avoided looking at Faith, even though she could feel her sister's glare boring holes in her head. Time seemed to inch by. When the bridal shower ended she felt drained. Keeping up pretenses hadn't been easy.

Pamela stayed downstairs to help her mother clean up, while Faith chased Stacey into her bedroom. The instant the door clicked shut Faith began interrogating her.

"Is he an actor? Because he sure acts as if he's in love with you."

"No, he's not an actor. He owns and runs Owens Technology."

"Why did he answer your ad, then?" Faith asked, not even trying to hide the suspicion in her voice.

"He didn't. The ad didn't work too well. I met him during an interview I was conducting for the newspaper. He heard about my situation and offered his help."

"What does he want out of this?"

"A few business contacts." Stacey lay on the bed on her stomach and buried her face in a pillow. "What am I going to do?" Her words came out muffled.

"You have only one choice. Tell everyone the truth."

Stacey lifted her head and gazed at her sister. "I can't. It would kill Mom and Dad. They love him."

"What about you?" Faith said. She looked at the two suitcases. "You're sharing a room together?"

Stacey rolled her eyes. "Nothing has happened and nothing will. I hired him for this weekend. After that, it's over and done with. I'll tell Mom and Dad the truth later."

Faith shook her head. "I don't think you're making the right choice, but it's your life and your responsibility. I'm not going to interfere."

Lance opened the door, then hesitated. "Am I interrupting something?"

"No." Faith frowned. "I was just leaving." As she reached the door, she turned back to Stacey and said, "Remember what I said."

Stacey nodded before dropping her head back on the pillow and closing her eyes. She listened to the door close and Lance's heavy footsteps moving around the room.

"What was that all about?" he asked.

"I told her."

A heavy pause settled in the room before he said, "You did, huh?"

"Yeah." Stacey turned on her side, her arm propped so her head could rest in her hand, and looked at him. Her stare met the blue depths of his eyes. "She thinks I should tell my parents the truth."

"And?"

"And I told her what I told you, I can't." Wanting only to change the subject, she asked, "What are you doing?"

"Taking a shower. You want to join me?" He lifted his brows as a sly grin crossed his lips.

A warmth spread from the pit of Stacey's

stomach and went in every direction. Heat rose in her cheeks.

"After all, we're married, remember?"

"How can I forget?"

Lance chuckled. "Your father told me the names he's picked out for our firstborn. He hopes it's a boy."

This situation had become more complicated then she had ever anticipated.

"I'm partial to Lance, Junior, myself," Lance said.

She groaned, and planted the pillow over her face.

For the party, Stacey dressed in a delicate silk white dress and pulled her hair up in a chignon. Diamonds adorned her ears and neck. She applied her makeup expertly. She'd been to many of these types of parties and knew exactly how to look and act, and what to say. Tonight all eyes would be on her and her new husband.

A knot formed in the pit of her stomach and seemed to be growing to the size of Mt. Rainier. So many things could go wrong this evening, and she'd thought over and over about every one of them. Her adrenaline raced. A light coat of perspiration covered her face no matter how much powder she used. She had to compose herself, appear confident in front of her family and friends. This evening would be the performance of her life.

As she slipped her shoes on she gazed over at Lance. A familiar warmth spread to her limbs at the handsome sight he made.

Lance turned and ran a glance over her. "You look beautiful."

"You look pretty good yourself."

"Shall we?" He held his arm out for her and met her at the door.

Many guests had already arrived when they descended the stairs. A man, who appeared to be drinking heavily in the corner of the room, caught Stacey's eye. Unconsciously her hand tightened on Lance's arm, and he followed her gaze. "You know him?"

Without looking at Lance she said, "Let me take care of him."

At the foot of the stairs Stan approached them. "Lance, there's a few people I'd like you to meet."

Stacey smiled and nodded, then walked away, leaving Lance in her father's hands. Halfway across the room Stacey ran into her mother. "Why did you invite Marc Newell?"

"I didn't," Carol said. "He just showed up. I couldn't exactly turn him away at the door."

Before she could say another word, Stacey's aunt and uncle came over to congratulate her. By the time she looked in Marc's direction again, he was gone. Thirty minutes passed before Lance rejoined her, slipped his arm around her waist, and played the part of doting husband.

Several times throughout the night Stacey had to remind herself that this marriage wasn't real. Tomorrow everything would return to normal once Lance drove her back home to South Sound. She felt like Cinderella at the ball, with Lance as Prince Charming, and at the stroke of midnight she would turn back into herself—single, with only a career to call her own. An emptiness settled inside her at the thought.

"Is everything all right?" Lance asked.

"Fine. You're doing a great job." She tried to smile, but only a weak one formed.

"Maybe it's not a job to me any more."

"What do you . . ."

"Attention, everyone," Stan said as he

tapped a spoon on his glass. "We have a couple of surprises for the happy couple tonight. First, I'd like to ask Stacey and Lance to come over here." As they came over the group of fifty people gathered around. Stan continued. "As most of you know I've been waiting for one of my daughters to marry for some time now. So this occasion pleases me very much. Stacey has chosen a good man, one we really like. I feel as if Lance is the son I never had."

Each word weighed heavily on Stacey. She felt as if she was in quicksand, sinking rapidly, with no branches in sight to grab onto. Soon, she would be in over her head.

"As a wedding gift to Stacey and Lance, her mother and I want to give them these." He handed each one a key. "Those are keys to a house we bought for you."

The guests applauded. Lance grinned, his brows raised in surprise.

Stacey groaned inwardly. She had to tell them. This was way out of hand now. Summoning all her courage, she said, "Dad, I have something to say."

"Just a minute, Stacey. I want to say something first, to all of you here tonight, our closest friends and family. As you know, I have been diagnosed with cancer. And, well, when I first heard the news I couldn't believe it. I became depressed." He shrugged. "I wanted to give up. How would I possibly continue running at the fast pace I do, and fight this disease at the same time? But then, when Stacey told me the good news, and we met Lance, my entire outlook on life changed. By God, I'm going to be here to see my first grandchild. I am so proud of Stacey. And Lance, you are the answer to my prayers."

Carol dabbed at the tears rolling down her cheeks. Many sniffs could be heard around the room.

"Hey, what's all this crying about? This is a celebration," Stan said, then turned to Stacey. "What did you want to say?"

The room fell silent. She could feel every pair of eyes on her. "I . . . I wanted to say . . ." The second she looked into her parents eyes, so filled with love and happiness, her courage dwindled. ". . . thank you." Her father and mother embraced and kissed her, then hugged Lance.

"You really shouldn't have done this," Lance said.

"You don't have to thank me, son." Stan

rested his hand on Lance's shoulder. "I just want you kids to get off to a good start, and maybe fill those extra bedrooms with children soon." The guests laughed.

Stacey's heart thudded in her chest. If this was the first surprise, she wasn't looking forward to the second one.

"The next surprise," Stan said, "is for the entire group. Since we missed out on seeing you two get married, we were hoping you would say your vows here tonight."

Chapter Four

Stacey could feel the blood drain from her face. Her breathing became short and shallow, her knees turned to Jell-O.

"I've asked Reverend White to join us tonight."

"Dad, we're really putting Stacey and Lance on the spot," Faith said, rushing the words out.

"Oh, Stacey," Carol said, a pleading tone in her voice. "Please do this for us. All my life I dreamed of helping you plan your wedding, and seeing you say your vows. Please, honey?"

Stacey couldn't think straight, let alone figure out what to say.

Faith stepped forward. "I really must object."

"Why on earth would you object?" Stan's voice rose, and his jaw muscle twitched. "This may be the only chance your mother and I get to see one of our daughters married. Why are you trying to deny us that?" A vein on his forehead became prominent.

"We are putting them on the spot, and it isn't fair," Faith persisted.

Stacey hadn't seen her sister's and father's strong wills collide in years. When they did, the house usually became a war zone.

"You know what I'm facing in a few weeks," Stan said. "Let me and your mother enjoy this moment."

Lance raised his hands in front of him, palms out like trying to quiet a crowd. "It's all right. We'd love to, Mr. Williams. Right, Stacey?"

Her mouth moved, but no words came out. What could she do?

Lance kept a loving smile on his lips as he gazed at her like a man in love, and led her to the bottom of the staircase. Reverend White stood on the step above them.

Stacey glanced at the crowd of people. Her parents wore happy smiles, her mother's eyes already filled with tears. Everybody appeared happy, except Faith, whose arms were crossed over her chest, her lower lip protruding in a pout and her nostrils flaring.

Lance turned and faced Stacey, taking her hands into his as if he had done this a million times before.

When she looked into his eyes she didn't see a bit of nervousness, anger, resentment, or disgust. She had gotten him into this jam—hired him, no less—to pose as her husband, and now she had just dug them deeper into a hole. At this rate they would be in China soon!

How could Lance be so calm? Her hands shook so badly he had to grip them extra tight to keep them steady.

Though the Reverend spoke, Stacey didn't hear a word he said. She couldn't. Her heart pounded too loudly. All of a sudden the Reverend paused. Lance squeezed her hands. First she darted a look at him, then the Reverend. Reverend White smiled in understanding, and reiterated the words she was supposed to say aloud. Slowly, mechanically, Stacey repeated them. With confidence, Lance took his turn, finishing the last word and squeezing her hands.

"You may kiss the bride," Reverend White said.

Lance pulled her into his arms and kissed her. The kiss was much more than a simple peck on the lips. When they broke apart he said for all to hear, "I love you."

Stacey searched his eyes. Darn, he was a good liar. She even started to believe him. As the taste of his kiss lingered on her lips, her heartbeat increased. She wondered what he would expect tonight as part of their "arrangement." The thought went tingling through her, yet at the same time she knew she would never give herself to this man, no matter how attracted she was to him. A deep love and commitment had to be there, the kind that made their vows more than words.

They stepped from the stairs and received more hugs from her parents, family members, and friends. By the time Stacey had hugged the last person in the room, she needed to be alone. She needed time to absorb what had just happened, and what she would do about it. Sneaking out of the house, she stepped out onto the back deck.

The cold air did little to cool the heat of desperation inside her. A full moon glistened high in the sky. She stood by the edge of the lighted pool and gazed at the steam rising up in a lazy fashion.

"I can't believe you went through with this farce of a marriage," a voice said behind her.

Stacey sucked in her breath and pivoted around. From the shadows, Marc Newell staggered out. His muscular build made up for his lack of height; he was only a couple inches taller than she. His thick, curly black hair and dark brown eyes made him look dangerous. His temper made him explosive. And right now, he was furious.

From three feet away she could smell the whiskey on his breath. Her heart raced in alarm. Did he know about what she had done? She would play it safe and act dumb.

"Marc," she said a little too breathlessly. "What are you talking about?"

He seized her arm and squeezed.

"You're hurting me," Stacey said.

"Yeah, well join the club. How could

you do this to me? How long have you known that guy? A whole month?"

"I told you it was over between us."

"You've humiliated me. I'm the laughing stock of your father's company."

"You shouldn't have come tonight." She pulled her arm free.

"Do you really know who you married?" Marc rushed on. "Of course you don't. That's Randolph Owens, and coincidentally enough, he just happens to be in the same business as your father."

"So what?"

He snorted. "Can't you see he married you for your father's business? He doesn't love you. All he sees are dollar signs."

"He has money. He doesn't need my father's." Stacey didn't know why she defended Lance. She hardly knew the man. Maybe she was just trying to protect herself.

"Why can't you see the big mistake you've made? I'm the one who loves you, not him."

"It's over between us. I'm married now."

"No! I'll never give you up. Just as I will never give up until I prove to you that

Owens married you to get his hands on your father's company."

The kitchen door clicked shut. They both turned.

Lance approached. He placed his arm around Stacey's waist, and met Marc's glare. "I don't believe we've met." He extended his hand. "Lance Owens. And you are?"

"Marc Newell. I'm Stan's right-hand-man, and a very close friend of Stacey's." Mark hesitated before he met Lance's grip.

"So you're in the computer business too," Lance said in a friendly tone.

As hard as Stacey tried, she couldn't ease the tension in her body. First getting married, and now having to deal with Marc. She wanted to run away, return to the small quiet town of South Sound and pretend this was all a bad dream.

"Yes. I've been in it many years. In fact, I worked my way up in Stan's company, and I don't intend on leaving any time soon."

Marc was looking for a fight. He got this way every time he drank too much. "I think it's time we returned to the party," Stacey said.

"Good idea." Lance smiled at her. "People were asking where you had gone." He directed her to the door.

"Don't forget what I said," Marc called out.

Stacey never formed a smile, only nodded at Marc before Lance opened the door for her and followed her in.

"What was that all about?" Lance asked.

"Don't worry about it—I'll handle Marc."

"Like you handled everything else?"

She whirled around and narrowed a stare at him. "I'm sorry I got us into this. Somehow I'll get us out. Just let me take care of Marc."

"I think I should take care of Marc," Lance said.

"You don't know him like I do."

"I know his type. He's a sore loser."

"He thinks you're after my father's company."

Lance forced a laugh. "And I suppose he intended to marry you for love." His sarcasm was loud and clear.

She tilted her head, her stare turning into suspicion. "To be honest, I really don't know what your motivation is, either."

Lance's eyes turned cold. He folded his arms over his chest. "I just saved your hind, remember? You're not showing much gratitude."

"Are you threatening me?"

A genuine laugh rumbled from him. "You know me better than that."

"That's the problem. I don't know you at all."

"Maybe you should have done better research, then." He moved passed her.

She watched him until the swinging door blocked him from her vision. His comment cut, and cut deep. The problem was that he was right, and that fact irritated her more than anything else. She had bungled this situation right from the get-go. And why?

She had to admit, at first her intentions were purely selfish. She had wanted to get her father off her back. But now her reasons had changed. Seeing her parents so happy, especially her father, and seeing how her marriage to Lance had changed her father's attitude and made him want to overcome his cancer, had altered the circumstances.

If she told them the truth now they would be devastated. Who knows what that would do to her father? Was there an answer to her problems? At this point there sure didn't appear to be one. Maybe, somehow, the problem would resolve itself. But how? And how long would Lance be willing to go along with this charade, especially once he got the contacts he needed for his business?

She sighed. Only time would tell.

Lance headed straight for the bar set up in the corner of the living room. The bartender poured him a cola. Lance took a sip of his drink, turned, leaned against the bar, and scanned the room. Stacey approached a group of ladies and began chatting with them. He stared at her until she looked at him. Color rose in her cheeks before she glanced away and ignored him, acting interested in what one of the women said.

Stan joined him. He glanced across the room at his daughter, then back to Lance. Stan ordered an iced tea. The two men didn't look at each other while they talked.

"I just met Marc Newell," Lance said, cursing the jealousy that knotted his stomach.

Stan took a sip, then said, "He meant

nothing to her. Their relationship was one-sided. I think it was more in Marc's mind than anything."

"So tell me, does she have any more old boyfriends here tonight?"

Stan laughed. "No. No more old boyfriends."

"Come with me." Stan motioned for Lance to follow, and led him into his office, shutting the door behind them. He stepped over to the desk and picked up a black pen that sat next to an official-looking document.

Lance drew his brows together. "What's this?"

"Your marriage license. The minister already signed it. I need your signature and Stacey's."

He took the pen from Stan, leaned over the desk, and scribbled his signature on it.

"I'm going to have it framed for both of you since Stacey couldn't find the original license."

"The original license," Lance repeated.

Stan slightly reddened. "I wasn't supposed to tell you, but when I asked Stacey to bring your marriage license she said she had lost it."

"I didn't know that."

"Yeah, well, pretend like you still don't. We don't need her mad at both of us." Stan chuckled. "Shall we join the party?"

Lance remained fixed next to the desk. "Mr. Williams."

Stan paused at the door, and pivoted to face Lance, a note of concern on his face. "Is something the matter, son?"

"Mr. Williams." At Stan's gesture of protest Lance said, "Stan. I really admire and respect you. Before I started my business I researched many companies in this field, and yours stood out among all the others. Not just for the quality of your products, but also for the way you ran your business."

A warm, endearing smile crossed Stan's face. "Thank you, Lance."

"That's why I have to be honest with you now. I respect you too much to lie to you."

Stan frowned. "You haven't been honest with me? About what?"

"About Stacey and me. We barely know each other."

Stan gave a hearty chuckle, strolled over to Lance, and slapped him on the shoulder.

"We all feel that way when we first get married."

"Yes, but—"

"Marriage and commitment are scary for men. There will be days when you'll think you were insane to have gone through with it, and then there will be days when you thank God you found such a deep love with her."

"You don't understand—"

The door opened, halting the conversation. Carol poked her head in. "Stan Williams. You should know better than to hog Lance from us—he still hasn't met all the family members."

"I was having him sign the marriage certificate. Stacey needs to sign it yet."

Carol nodded. Leaving the door open, she retrieved Stacey.

Stacey entered the room, her questioning glanced directed at Lance.

"We need you to sign this," Stan said, moving behind the desk and picking up the pen.

Stacey stood next to her father, her face turning pale as she gazed upon the document.

Lance took this moment to study the

pure lines of her profile. Strands of hair had fallen out of her chignon, making her appear even more beautiful. What man wouldn't want her?

My goodness, she's my wife.

He might have only known her for a few days, but she was constantly on his mind. Last night he couldn't sleep, knowing she was beside him and yet a world away.

Tonight would be no different.

This marriage certificate meant nothing to her. But he felt differently. Since they had met, she filled his thoughts every waking moment of the day. The gentle curve of her face, the deep green of her eyes, her adorable dimple. He wanted to reach out and run his fingers through her hair, its texture so soft and silky.

The talk they had shared during their walk on the beach had connected them. She touched something deep inside him, a need for friendship, for someone to care about him, for someone he could trust—needs he never knew he had until he met her. She was special, different, unlike any other woman he had known. Stacey was the type of woman any man would feel lucky to have as his wife. Even though she had lied to her parents, her intentions were noble. As crazy as it seemed, this was her way of trying to help.

Sylvia would never have gone to such lengths to help anyone, not even her own family. Lance didn't know too many people that would.

One thing he knew for sure was that life with Stacey would never be boring—that he could count on.

The evening seemed to drag on for Stacey. Before the last guest left, she climbed the stairs to their bedroom. Minutes later Lance came in, which didn't surprise her much. Why did he go through with this marriage? He had been such a good sport about it all. Maybe *too* good of a sport.

She went into the bathroom, put on her sweats, brushed her teeth, and washed her face. When she came out she found Lance sitting on the side of the bed, his legs outstretched, wearing an undershirt and black pants, and staring at his bare feet. A curl of hair drooped down over his forehead. He looked like a model posing for an ad.

"It's all yours," she said, trying to sound carefree, hoping he wouldn't notice how the sight of him could make her heart beat louder than the pounding drums of a rock 'n' roll band.

He didn't move.

"Lance?"

He glanced up at her, his expression serious, sober. "We need to talk."

She sighed. Suddenly it struck her why he'd been acting so strange. The cold realization of marriage had set in. He probably thought marrying her had been a big, huge mistake.

"I know what's wrong," she said.

"You do?"

"Sure. You're angry with me for not coming forth with the truth." She lifted her shoulders. "I can't really blame you."

He frowned, opened his mouth to speak, then stopped himself.

"Look, I know we're in a jam, but somehow I'll get us out of this. Just give me a little more time."

"If I give you any more time we'll probably have a dozen children by then." Lance laughed at his own joke.

She rolled her eyes, then sat next to him on the bed and placed her hand on his. "I'm grateful for all you've done. Most men would have lost their cool and blurted the truth out to everyone. Thank you for not humiliating my family like that."

Lance stared at her hand on his before he met her eyes, then he dropped his gaze to her lips. Even though he cleared his throat his voice still came out husky. "This whole situation is so crazy, maybe we should be crazy with it. Maybe we should keep together . . ."

Was he going to kiss her? She wanted him to. She wanted him to kiss her the way he did after they had said, "I do." What would it be like to run her fingers over his muscular shoulders, or to feel him kiss her neck . . .

"—give this marriage a try," Lance finished saying.

"What?" She looked at him as if he had lost his mind. Maybe he had.

"I said, maybe we should try to make this marriage work."

"That's the stupidest idea I've ever heard! We've only known each other two days."

"Technically its been longer than that."

She forced out a breath and shook her head. A thought struck her and her eyes narrowed in on him. "You *are* after my father's business, aren't you? Marc was right about you, wasn't he?"

Lance's face seemed to turn to stone, and his eyes took on an icy, distant appearance. "Forget it, Stacey. Forget I even suggested it." He pushed off the bed and went into the bathroom, shutting the door with a firm click.

She had wounded his pride and attacked his integrity, all in an effort to push him away. He had been nothing but nice, kind, gentle, and understanding. She would miss talking to him and being with him after they returned to South Sound. He was more like a friend than any friend she'd ever had, male or female.

She sprawled on the bed, lying on her back, placed her hands under her head, and stared up at the ceiling. After several minutes Lance came out, turned the lights off, and climbed into bed. She glanced over at him. He rested on his side, his back to her.

"I'm sorry," she whispered.

His head slightly turned toward her, then rolled back onto his pillow.

He wouldn't even talk to her. Here she

was afraid of what he might expect of her tonight—nothing to fear now. He couldn't stand the sight of her. Well, this clinched it. She's in China now.

They packed Lance's sedan with as many wedding gifts as they could carry, and still couldn't get them all in. Stacey's parents promised to visit in a week and bring the rest of them down.

"Oh, I forgot to tell you kids something," Stan said. "Stacey, while you've been here I hired a moving company to move your stuff into your new house. Everything is waiting for you there. I told your landlord you wouldn't be coming back."

"You what?" Stacey asked.

"You don't have to thank me." Stan beamed with pride.

Stacey was too tired to argue the point right now, not having slept all night. She yawned before she gave her mother, father, and sisters hugs goodbye. "Thanks for everything."

"We enjoyed doing it for you, honey," Carol said.

"As soon as you get your phone in, give

me a call," Faith said, and emphasized her words with a hard glare.

"Will do." They got into the car, waved goodbye, and drove away. Silent tension filled the car. Stacey wanted to sleep, but she couldn't because the pile of presents in the back prevented her seat from lowering. She yawned again.

"If you'd like you can put your head on my lap," Lance said.

Stacey eyed him.

He chuckled, but it lacked a genuine humor. "Haven't I already proved to you I don't bite?"

"I never thought you would." She rested her head on his leg and could feel the muscles tighten, loosen, then tighten again as he switched from the gas pedal to brake and back again. After several minutes she drifted to sleep.

Lance couldn't remember when his hand first dropped and stroked her hair. He didn't even realize he was doing it until he began to twist the soft strands around his finger. How many times did he glance down at her while they crossed on the ferry, then drove south? Too many to count. Each time he looked at her a warmth spread through his limbs.

How had she managed to capture his heart so quickly? Unfortunately, she didn't feel the same about him. It stung when she had accused him of wanting her father's company.

Several times he wondered if his feelings for Stacey were nothing more than a rebound from Sylvia, recovering his pride. Yet each time that thought popped in his mind, his gut told him differently.

Looking back, he realized his relationship with Sylvia had been more out of convenience than love. Something had always been missing. A deeper connection, a genuine caring about another human being, and a love that went beyond the physical.

Relief washed over him like a warm waterfall pouring over his head. Life with Sylvia would have been a big mistake, and undoubtedly ended in divorce. She might have been a brilliant lawyer and a beautiful woman, but she lacked depth. All he would have ever had with her was a surface relationship, and he wanted more than that. Much more. He wanted someone to share his life with. Someone to care about the most trivial things in his life, to care about how his day went. Someone he could talk to about his business and who would understand what he was saying. Most of all, he wanted someone he could start a family with. Now in his early thirties, Lance didn't want to wait too much longer to be a father.

He glanced at Stacey again, and briefly followed the curve of her chin before returning his eyes to the road. What would their children look like? Probably beautiful just like her, with her proud chin, the one she threw up at him each time she became defensive. He smiled. While she slept there was a softness about her that stirred something deep inside him, something that was much more than desire.

With determination Lance decided he would make this marriage work. Fate had brought them together for a reason. They were meant for each other, whether she knew it or not. Somehow he would get her to see that.

The gray cloudy sky made for a long drive back to South Sound. Stacey pulled out written instructions to the house and read them aloud to Lance. The directions took them away from town and out into the country. They turned down a long driveway, and silently stepped out of the car and gazed upon the large white structure.

They entered through the front door. The living room was on one side, an expansive unfurnished room, done in pale peach wallpaper and white molding. The fireplace stood out with a white and gray marble inset and teakwood mantel, delicately carved in a fan design.

A wide open doorway led into a formal dining room, large enough to seat at least twelve. Beautiful floral fabric in blues, pinks, and greens accented the walls, and an off-white rug covered most of the dark hardwood floor.

They wandered through the house and discovered it had five bedrooms. A slight hint, no doubt, from her father. The last room they came to upstairs was the master bedroom, the only room furnished with new furniture in the house. The white walls and braided rug emphasized the white, red, pink, and green floral design of the bedspread, curtains, and couch. Bamboo and wicker pieces of furniture enhanced the lightness of the room.

They finished the tour, ending up downstairs opposite the living room in the library, where bookshelves lined three of the four walls.

"This room will be large enough to run my business out of until I get my new building built," Lance said.

Stacey cast him a questioning glance. "You're not planning on living here, are you?"

Lines formed on his forehead. "Of course. Most married couples do live together."

"We're not really married."

"Yes we are. You signed the marriage license just as I did. And I remember you saying, 'I do.' "

"I didn't have a choice."

Lance placed his finger under her chin and tipped her head up so she met his gaze. "You always have a choice in life. You made yours. Live with it."

She jerked her head away. "I've also made the choice to right this situation . . . somehow." As she left the office, she paused to look at the boxes of her belongings piled high against one wall in the living room. "For now you can stay wherever you've been staying," Stacey announced.

Lance stepped from the office, his arms crossed over his chest. "Stacey, don't do this. I'm tired of sleeping on the couch in that dirty office building. Besides, you need me here."

She forced a sharp breath out. "I need you? Here?" She knew she did, but her pride prevented her from begging him to continue to play his part. She would wait until she became much more desperate to do that.

"Up 'til now, I've been more than co-operative. I've gone beyond the call of duty. I've played the part of your husband and convinced your family and friends. I know that you love your family so much you would get yourself in trouble like this just to make them happy." His glance ran the length of her body and back up. He lifted his brows. "I could have put all kinds of conditions on our arrangement, but I haven't."

Her face reddened as his gaze rested on her lips. Then he glanced away. "We're *going* to live in this house together. Have you forgotten your parents are coming down in a week? What would they say if I wasn't here?"

She knew he was right, but darn it anyway, she didn't want him to be. All she wanted was to be out of this predicament. If she lived with Lance she would undoubtedly start to become dependent upon him, whether it was for friendship, or more than that. She had to prove to herself, to her family, and especially to her father that she could make it on her own, that she was an independent woman who could make it in a career of her choice with no one's help.

She straightened her shoulders and lifted her chin. "Fine, but I get the bed. I'm not sharing a bed with you again."

"And I'm not sleeping on the hard floor."

Stacey lifted her brows. "Not tough enough to take it, huh?"

He folded his arms over his chest. "No, I'm not stupid enough to take it." He sighed. "Tomorrow I'll move your furniture in from the garage and sleep on your couch. Okay?"

"It's a deal."

"It's always a deal with us, isn't it?"

She tilted her head and frowned.

"Never mind."

With a shrug, she headed out to the car to retrieve their gifts. She had to keep her mind off of Lance. How would she get through another night with him? Yanking on the handle to the backseat door, she found it locked, along with all the doors. She leaned against the car, her arms crossed over her chest.

Lance stood in the doorway watching her. He dangled the remote key from his fingers. "Need this?" He strolled to the car. Their shoulders lightly touched when he pressed the remote and released the lock. He grasped the handle, then paused. "Shouldn't I carry the bride over the threshold?" A chuckle rippled from his throat.

He opened the car door and hauled a load in the house. Stacey trailed behind him, her arms full of packages. Lance retrieved the remaining presents and luggage, then shut the front door. "I'm going to go into town to get my computer equipment. I figure if I work this far out of town, then no nosey newspaper reporter will bother me."

"Very funny."

*   *   *

While Lance packed up his computer equipment he couldn't get Stacey off his mind. She was an independent woman, yet she needed someone to look after her and keep her out of trouble. The fire in her green eyes contrasted with her softness and gentleness, the two qualities she tried to suppress, but would never be able to hide.

Lance suspected Stacey usually didn't lie, because she was so bad at it. She had gone to such lengths just to make her parents happy. A pressure tugged at his heart. He wished she wanted to make *him* happy. With a deep sigh he closed his eyes. Was he falling in love, so quickly? He wouldn't know—this would be a first for him.

Thoughts of Sylvia splashed in his mind. His feelings for her never came close to what he felt for Stacey right now. He couldn't imagine Sylvia ever advertising for a husband just to make someone happy, especially her parents. All she ever wanted was for someone to meet her needs, not the other way around, and that always left him empty. Closeness and intimacy had been missing from their relationship, an intimacy that allows the one you love to see you as you really are, and to know that you are loved for all your faults as well as your good qualities.

Lance took extra care loading his equipment into the car, then stopped for lunch. By the time he returned and set the computer up in the library, he was ready for bed. He shut the lights off and trudged up the stairs.

Stacey stepped out of the bathroom, wearing a pink silk nightgown and bathrobe.

Lance's breath caught. Quickly, he cleared his throat. "What happened to your sweats?"

"Don't get any ideas." She stepped over to the bed and pulled the covers down. "The sweats were too uncomfortable."

Lance retreated into the bathroom, shutting the door behind him. He splashed cold water on his face, then looked at himself in the mirror. "Get a grip," he mumbled. She looked like a beauty queen, the light accentuating her curves, her blond hair brushed until every strand shone, and her eyes such an incredible shade of green.

Lance dragged in a long, slow breath, then exhaled. Tonight he wouldn't be able to sleep as easily as he thought he would.

He might be exhausted from the weekend and the move, but right now adrenaline flowed through his body like a runaway train going downhill.

Lance took his time with his toiletries, hoping she would be asleep by the time he climbed into bed. Darn it. He had been raised to be a gentleman, and he had been so far . . . tonight would really test him.

The bed dipped as he climbed in. This bed was smaller then the one at her parents' house. He could feel her warmth as she lay inches from him. He turned over on his side, away from her. He hoped that by not seeing her it would cool his desires, but it only made them stronger, made his mind wander and wonder.

He had made many mistakes in his life, ones even worse than Stacey lying to her parents about being married. He didn't intend to make any now. He would take one day at a time and see what happened.

But tomorrow, first thing, he would go to the store and buy a bed, and put it in the room at the far end of the hall. Out of sight, out of mind, right? Somehow he doubted that old saying.

Chapter Five

The week passed quickly. Stacey buried herself in her work, as did Lance. Her nerves started to fray by the time Saturday arrived, and now her parents were due any minute. Now she and Lance had to suddenly become the loving newlyweds, when they had hardly spoken a word to each other all week.

The doorbell rang and Stacey hurried to answer it. She let her parents in, and immediately noticed her father looked pale and tired.

Her mother handed her a large wrapped box. "We got you a housewarming gift."

"That was hardly necessary, since you

gave me—us—the house." Her eyes darted to her parents, but they acted as if they hadn't heard her blunder.

Lance came out of his office, a wide smile creasing his lips. He held his hand out. "How are you doing, Mr. Williams, Mrs. Williams?" He nodded to Carol.

As Stan shook his hand he said, "Now what did I say about calling me Dad?"

Lance smiled. "I guess that'll take time."

Stan laughed. "Take all the time you need, son. After all, you have the rest of your life."

Despite her father's jovial behavior, Stacey detected something deeply troubling him and her mother. Could they have found out what she had done? Faith—Faith must have told them, her conscience getting the better of her.

"Would you like a tour of the house?" Lance asked.

"We'd love one," Stan said. "We went through a real estate agent, and he showed us the house and rooms on a computer."

"It was quite fun to shop that way," Carol said. "We were able to look at many more houses on the computer than if we'd had to visit each one."

"I thought this looked like a nice new development, one you could raise your children in without worrying too much about your neighbors."

Stacey rolled her eyes. First he nagged her about getting married, and now his latest topic was children. Good grief. "Dad, we'll have kids when we're ready. We just got married."

"My father always said, 'The time to have kids is when you're young.'" Stan glanced at Lance. "I bet your husband is more than ready to start a family. Am I right, Lance?"

"Actually I am ready."

Stacey glared at him, her lips squeezed together. "I'm not. And I'm the one that has to carry the baby, remember?"

Carol laughed. "Oh, Stacey. You always let your father get your goat."

"He has a way about him," Stacey muttered.

Lance led the way, showing Stan and Carol every room in the house, including the garage, while Stacey trailed behind. The tour ended in the living room, where Lance and Stan sat down on Stacey's couch. They chatted about the latest computer news, what the stock market was doing, and ideas they shared about future trends.

Stacey and her mother went into the kitchen. "I already made sandwiches, but I need to cut up the fruit."

"I'll help."

A dead silence hung in the kitchen as the women worked. Stacey finally said, "Dad's not looking too well."

A deep, exaggerated sigh escaped her mother's lips. "He won't slow down. You know your father—he thinks he's invincible."

"Has he scheduled the surgery yet?"

"No." Carol stopped cutting an orange and looked at Stacey. "I really wish you could get Lance to reconsider working at Microland. Your father's not a young man anymore, Stacey. He can't keep up this pace. And he's too proud to beg. I'm afraid he's going to kill himself."

"Mom—"

Carol held her hand up. "I know what you're going to say. I realize you two have your own careers. But honey, when you push everything aside, money, success, career—all you have left is family. That's all that matters in life. Your father has done so much for you and your sisters. Now it's time to give back."

"I'll think about it."

"And Stacey . . . think seriously about starting your family. I hate to rush you. But if your father's condition takes a turn for the worst, his dying wish would be to see his grandchild before he . . ."

"Mom, don't talk like that."

"Let me see what we have in here," Lance said, walking into the kitchen with Stan. Lance opened the refrigerator and peered inside. "I wasn't able to get to the grocery store this week . . . luckily Stacey found the time. We have soda, juice, or bottled water."

"I'll take a soda."

Lance grabbed two cans and returned with Stan into the living room.

Stacey followed them to the kitchen doorway. "Don't get too comfortable, guys," Stacey said. "We're almost ready to eat."

"Good. I'm starved," Lance said.

"You're always starved." Stacey shook her head.

Lance met her stare, raised his eyebrows, and gave her a devilish smile.

A tingling rose in Stacey's stomach. Lance looked so incredibly handsome when he smiled and flirted with her. He sure knew how to put on the charm when the need arose. She had never seen her father so taken with another man before. And Lance acted as if her father was his hero. If Lance gave her half the attention he gave her father, then maybe their marriage could—

Stacey stopped her thought process. Darn it. She missed Lance. She missed talking to him, being with him, even just seeing him. The house was so large they rarely crossed paths. Sometimes she wondered if he didn't keep himself locked in his office in an effort to avoid her.

"Where do you want me to put this?" Carol asked, holding a bowl of sliced apples and oranges.

"Oh, let's eat at the table in the breakfast nook." Stacey set the table, put out the food, and called everyone in.

A silence came over the room as they ate. Her father said, "You know, when your mother and I first started out we had practically nothing. And before we knew it Faith was on the way." He chuckled. "Boy, was she a big baby. Ten pounds, eleven ounces. And she was headstrong from birth."

"Gee, I wonder who she got that from," Stacey said, smiling.

"There's nothing like holding your first-born in your arms," Stan said, addressing Lance. "Maybe you'll have a son. But boy or girl, it doesn't matter. You still can play ball with them, hold them, and love them." He shifted his glance to Stacey. "They sure grow up fast. Before you know it they're married and having kids of their own."

Instead of her normal protest, Stacey said nothing. She couldn't help but feel she owed this to her father. He *had* done so much for her. He had taught her to play softball, basketball, and soccer. He had given her piano lessons, a car in high school, and a college education. But most of all, he had given her his love. He had dried her tears, and celebrated her joys. He had been her champion and protector, and always her teacher.

"You look far away," Lance said.

Stacey jerked her head in his direction. "Oh. I was just thinking."

"About a baby, I hope," Stan said.

"No, Dad. About a wonderful father."

As usual, he brushed off the compliment, and concentrated on his food.

The following week Stacey took the day off from work and drove into Seattle. By the time she returned home, the furniture she ordered had been delivered and was arranged in the living room. The white and forest green striped couch faced the fireplace, which at the moment had a fire burning in it. A coffee table sat in between the couch and fireplace, and green floral upholstered chairs were placed at each end. Finally, a comfortable place to sit down.

Stacey glanced at the book in her lap. Donors. The book was filled with possible candidates, men who didn't want to be involved in her child's life, which would create an uncomplicated situation, free from a messy divorce and painful tugs-of-war.

She had been embarrassed going into the center, and wore her sunglasses the entire time. Her heart nearly leaped out of her chest when she spotted a woman she thought she had recognized. Luckily, the woman had been a lookalike.

Removing her shoes, she curled her feet underneath her and opened to the first page. Placing her elbow on the arm of the couch, she rested the side of her head in her hand. She needed a donor to fit the profile of a man that her father would pick for her. She needed a man like—Lance. As if he had read her mind he entered the room.

"Where have you been? I called your office and they told me you took the day off. Is your father okay?" He not only sounded concerned, but he looked concerned.

"Yes. I went for a drive." She closed the book when he stepped further into the room and sat down beside her.

His gaze zeroed in on the black binder. "What's that?"

"Nothing." She answered quickly in a high-pitched voice.

His brows drew together before he reached out and lifted the book from her hands. He opened to the first page and scanned the bio of the first man. "What *is* this?"

She glanced away and mumbled, "Donors."

"What?"

Stacey could only meet his eyes for a second. As she snatched the book back, she said with a little more confidence, "Sperm donors." Opening the book and turning the pages, she acted absorbed in its contents.

"Are you're looking for a man to father your baby?" Lance crossed his arms over his chest. "Heck, I'll do that for free, and you're even married to me."

She stared at the page, the words blurred. She couldn't concentrate on words or pictures, not with Lance sitting so close, his shoulder bumping hers, his breath brushing her cheek, the warmth of his body so comforting.

"We're not really married." Darn, her words came out breathless, matching her erratic pulse and heartbeat.

"Sure we are." He ran his finger along her cheek, then pushed her hair back. His lips followed the same path. He smelled pleasant, a light fresh woody cologne. His face was cleanly smooth and shaven, rubbing against her skin.

Stacey stiffened, her head dizzy, her body tingling. "You make it sound so simple." She closed her eyes.

"It is simple if you'd let it be." His voice was near her ear. His hand gently grasped her chin and turned it. Soon his mouth covered hers.

For a moment she gave in to his touch, to the feel of his mouth, the rightness of it. Her reserve dwindled. He was seducing her, and she felt powerless to stop him. But she had to. This was part of his plot, to seduce her, and get her pregnant. Then and only then would his position in her father's company become secure.

She pulled back and had to catch her breath. "No. Stop. This isn't right."

Carefully, Lance drew air into his lungs and released it. "It felt pretty right to me."

Stacey stared at the book, her grip turning her knuckles white. She struggled to find her voice. "Don't you have work to do?" Heat rose in her cheeks and she couldn't look at him, yet she felt his penetrating stare.

"I'm stuck. I'm waiting for a friend to call."

"Oh, so you're just trying to amuse yourself until then." When she glanced at him she could tell she'd hurt his feelings.

He stood up and started to walk away,

then paused, turned and faced her. "By the way, I liked the article you wrote on the chemical company that's polluting the local river. It was well written and researched."

She hesitated before she said, "Thank you." After he left she sat and stared at the fire. Right now, she felt terrible. In an effort to defend herself against his advances she had insulted him and he'd returned the comment with a compliment, praise about her work, work that meant a lot to her.

She heard him leave through the back door. Stacey set the book aside, no longer interested in the donors. Standing up, she headed into the office, sat behind the computer, and stared at the screen. The code looked familiar. In fact, she'd used it when she had helped develop a software program for her father's company a year ago. Over the summer she and Marc had worked closely together on it—that's how they'd met. She closed her eyes, wishing she could forget that memory.

Stacey spent the next hour troubleshooting the error. Adrenaline began to pump through her veins. Code and programs were a challenge to her. They reminded her of a puzzle or riddle that she just *had* to solve. She knew she was good at it, too.

A sense of guilt niggled at her gut.

She probably *should* work for her father's company, but darn it, she wanted to do something on her own. All her life, her father told her what subjects to take in school, where to work, who to work for, and never once did he ask her what she wanted or what she was interested in. She had a creative side to her she wanted to explore.

"Ah," she said, spotting the error. Her fingers flew over the keys, punching in the correct code. Again, she ran the program. A satisfaction swept through her.

Problem solved.

"What are you doing?" Lance demanded, storming around the desk. Anger flushed his face. His eyes hardened to a steel blue. "I don't want you fooling around on this computer, ever." He stared at the screen. "It'll take me weeks to correct what you've done."

Stacey sat back in the chair and crossed her arms over her chest. "I *solved* your problem. A thank you will do nicely."

When she saw the doubt in his eyes she ran the program.

The muscles around his mouth and forehead relaxed. "How did you do that?"

She brought up the code and showed him the error.

He looked at her as if seeing her for the first time. Admiration and respect filled his eyes.

Stacey stood up, stepped aside, and gestured for him to sit in the chair. "It's all yours."

"It is?" In one swift move, he moved in front of her and gathered her into his arms. "I have to thank you properly." His mouth came down on hers and he kissed her with a passion she hadn't detected in his previous kisses. Stacey's mind whirled. She hadn't anticipated this move. He'd caught her off guard and she found herself responding to his kisses. He placed both his hands on the sides of her neck, then ran them down her arms to her waist. He lifted her up on the desk so her legs dangled at the knees.

Ring! Ring! Lance groaned.

"Let it go," Stacey said breathlessly.

Lance sighed. "I can't." He snatched the receiver. "Your timing is impeccable."

Stacey pushed off the desk.

Lance lifted his hand in a gesture of apology and regret. He mouthed the words, "Sorry."

She nodded in understanding and left the room, returning to the couch. She needed to regain her composure. Her heart still hadn't returned to normal. She sat on the couch and opened the book, once again, and combed through the pages. There had to be an acceptable donor in here somewhere. Or was the answer to her problem sitting in the office just a few feet away?

Chapter Six

"Stacey," her editor, Kyle Drew, called. "Let's go into my office and discuss your next assignment."

She nodded and followed him into a cluttered room. Papers were strewn about, several half-empty coffee cups sat on his desk, and a musty smell filled the room. She wondered how he could possibly function in such a jumbled mess. He gestured to a chair opposite his desk, but she had to move a stack of newspapers off it to sit down.

"So what's my next assignment?"

Kyle sat on the corner of his desk and pulled on the red suspenders that held up his jeans and pressed against his flannel shirt. From the first day she met Kyle she noticed he preferred comfort over appearance. He had told her that in a small town of farmers and loggers, what he wore really didn't matter much.

"Randolph Owens," he said.

Stacey crossed her legs and tugged at the tan skirt that matched her blazer and ivory silk blouse. She rapidly tapped her pencil against her pad, the beat matching the tempo of her heart. "Randolph Owens?"

"I'm wondering why you've dropped him as a story. The public loved your articles on him."

"Yeah, well, he's old news. Besides, he never gave me any information when I interviewed him."

"He will now."

She swallowed. "Why?"

"I got a tip." Kyle stood, traveled around the desk, and leaned against it. "He's negotiating a merger with Microland. And they may be building a new branch here in South Sound. Can you believe the number of jobs it would bring to this depressed economy?"

Stacey rose out of her seat and crossed

the small room to the table, pivoted, and folded her arms over her chest. The entire time she had worked at the newspaper Stacey had purposefully withheld the fact that Stan Williams was her father. She wanted to earn this job on her own merits, and had.

"Sounds like rumors to me," she said.

"They're not rumors. I want you to track him down and get a quote."

"Who'd you hear this from?"

Kyle drew his bushy brows together. "A reliable source."

"Does this source have a name?"

Kyle hesitated. "Yes."

"And it is?"

"Confidential."

"Why are you being so secretive about this person?"

"Why are you so curious about him?" Kyle returned to his chair.

Stacey hustled to the front of his desk, braced her arms on the edge, and leaned forward. "So it's a him?"

Kyle forced a long breath out. "Yes. It's a him. Now let it go."

"How do you know this person is telling the truth? It could be anyone off the street, wanting attention or money."

"I'm not paying him."

"Then why's he telling you? What does he want out of it?"

"I don't know. I didn't ask him."

"I bet he doesn't even know Lan—Randolph Owens, or anyone at Microland."

"Trust me. This guy knows."

"Does he work for Microland?"

Kyle's face and neck turned a darker shade of red, and his eyes narrowed. He jabbed his finger in the air at her. "Verify the story with Owens."

She pushed away, and turned to leave.

"Oh," Kyle said. "I'm getting heat from county officials on the chemical plant story. So unless you can come up with concrete evidence they're dumping hazardous waste into the river, you're going to have to drop the story."

She whirled around. "Since when have you caved in to pressure?"

"Well, maybe I'm just getting too old for this business." Kyle went back to reading the document in front of him.

Stacey wasn't sure what he meant by his comment, but right now she wouldn't press the issue. She had other things on her mind, like who was feeding Kyle these bogus rumors. Or were they true? Had Lance negotiated a deal with her father and not told her?

Stacey returned to her desk. For the next hour she worked on an article about the school levy, and how the money would help improve the decaying buildings. She had almost finished when Kyle stopped by her desk.

"I forgot to tell you that Wanda's off this week, so you'll have to cover her story, too."

"What's she covering?" Stacey said with a groan.

"She was supposed to get dirt on Owens' sudden marriage. I heard he married some woman in town after knowing her for only a week. Find out who the woman is. Get a quote from her too. Better yet, get a picture of her." Kyle wore a sly grin, like he had given her the story of the year. "People love this stuff. And I intend to make it front page news."

"Do you really think it's necessary to delve into a person's personal life? Shouldn't it remain private?"

Kyle narrowed his stare at her. "What's gotten into you? For weeks you've been attacking this man in the newspaper because he wouldn't talk to you. Now you're worried about his privacy?" He shook his head.

"It's not ethical to expose a person's private life to the world."

On a sigh he said, "Yeah, well, ethical or not, it's what sells newspapers nowadays, and that's what we're in business to do. Now, I'm giving you this assignment because you're my best reporter. If you don't think you can do it—"

"I can do it," she said quickly. "I'll get on it right away."

Stacey left work early and drove straight home. She dumped her coat and purse on the couch and went into the kitchen. She grabbed a soda from the refrigerator and opened it.

"So how was your day, dear?" Lance said, sitting at the kitchen table, a notepad in front of him.

Stacey gasped. "I didn't see you there." She moved around the counter and sat across from him. "What are you doing?"

"Making a menu and grocery list."

"You know how to cook?" She sounded surprised.

"A little. I used to eat out a lot when I lived in California. I don't have that luxury now, starting my business over. So I'll have to brush up on my culinary skills. Any requests?"

"Hmm. Let me think . . . how about stroganoff?"

"Stroganoff it is. Oh, by the way, I washed the clothes today. Yours are folded on your bed."

Her mouth opened. "Wow. Thanks. You cook *and* clean. I just might keep you around after all."

Lance grinned. "I hope so." His stare met hers.

Stacey's glanced dropped to her soda can. "You wouldn't believe the assignment I was given today."

"Oh?"

She flipped the metal tab on the can back and forth until it came off, then looked at Lance. "I've been ordered to interview Randolph Owens, and find out if the rumor is true that he's merging with Microland."

"You're kidding, right?"

"I wish I was. Worse yet—Kyle heard Randolph Owens got married, and I'm supposed to interview his wife."

"Well, that won't be hard. Why didn't you tell your boss you married me?"

"And have to answer all his questions?" She shook her head. "I don't think so. Besides, Kyle doesn't know I'm related to the owner of Microland." When Lance frowned she shrugged and added, "I wanted to get this job on my own merit. Not because of who I'm related to."

Lance nodded. "I understand."

"Really?"

"I felt the same way with my father. That's why I went into a completely different field."

She smiled. "I guess that's another thing we have in common."

Lance changed the subject. "So who's your boss getting his information from?"

"I wish I knew. He wouldn't tell me."

"Maybe you already know."

She tilted her head. "Who?"

"Marc."

"I thought of him. But I can't imagine him doing something like this. What would he have to gain?"

Lance shrugged. "Who knows? Maybe it's his way of trying to come between us."

"I don't see how it would."

"I think only time will tell what he's up to. Until then, what are you going to do?"

"Stall. And focus on another project I've been working on."

"Which is?"

The phone rang. She held up a finger. "Saved by the bell." Stacey hurried over and snatched the receiver. She had contacted people who lived near the chemical plant and asked them to call her if they suspected something was going on.

An elderly lady Stacey had made friends with asked, "Is Stacey Williams there?"

"This is she."

"This is Gretchen Towne. Remember, we spoke earlier?"

"Yes, of course, Gretchen. What can I do for you?"

Gretchen lowered her voice. "I heard my son talking. He works at the plant."

"I remember."

"He said he had to work really late tonight, because the plant had a special project for him to work on."

"Do you think they're dumping tonight?"

"Possibly." Gretchen paused. "I—I don't want to hurt my son. He needs his job. But what they are doing is wrong. I live downstream and I've lost five dairy cows in the last two months alone. I can't afford to lose more."

"I understand. There are other ways the plant can handle these matters."

"I know I can trust you. You're such a sweet girl."

Stacey smiled. "Thank you."

"Keep me posted. And remember, you didn't hear this from me."

"Of course." Stacey hung up the phone and stared into space. How should she handle this situation? Kyle said he wanted evidence. She didn't have a choice. She would have to get evidence, hard evidence. And that was exactly what she intended to do.

"Who was that?" Lance asked.

She jerked her head in his direction. "Oh, uh, somebody from work."

Lance dropped the subject, which Stacey was thankful for. Right now, she had more important things to think about than answering questions.

Stacey suspected the chemical company had been dumping illegally for a long time, but she could never get the photographs or documentation she needed to expose them. Tonight, with camera in hand, she would finally catch them in the act. Pictures never lied.

She checked her watch: 11:00. Minor Chemical Company always waited to dump until the early morning hours. That's why no one ever caught them, especially since the plant was located far out of town, surrounded by acres of abandoned farmland and woods.

A slight satisfaction filled her and brought a smile to her face. Her father said she'd never get a good story reporting in a small farming and logging community—how wrong he was!

Slipping on a pair of black jeans, a black sweatshirt, and a pair of sneakers, she tied her hair back in a ponytail, loaded her camera, and patted her pocket for extra film. She tip-toed down the stairs and out of the house, afraid to breathe for fear Lance would hear her. The last thing she needed was for him to find out what she was up to, and try to talk her out of it.

A reporter had to do what a reporter had to do.

Stacey drove far out into the country and parked her car behind a group of bushes. She crossed the street and peered through the tall chainlink fence. In the distance, bright floodlights glowed over an area near the river. She could hear engines roar as they loaded barrels onto large trucks. She snapped a few pictures, and decided to head south. She followed the sharp bend in the road, and walked quite a distance to get a better shot.

Adrenaline pumped through her veins as the dumping site came into view. *This was the spot.* She had them. Finally. She zeroed in on the action taking place with her zoom lens. As soon as the roll ran out she reloaded, slipped the used film in her pocket, then waited and watched.

"What are you doing?" someone whispered behind her.

Stacey gasped, whipped around, then relaxed when she recognized Lance. "I should be asking *you* that question."

"I heard you leave, and I thought an emergency must have come up with your father. So I followed you."

She'd been so focused on getting the pictures she hadn't noticed anyone following her here.

Lance stepped closer to her in the deep grass. "Do you realize how late it is?"

She nodded to the trucks. "They're dumping toxic waste into the river." She patted her camera. "I've got it all here." Turning back, she said, "If I could only get a little closer . . ."

"Are you crazy?"

Ignoring him, she scaled the six foot chainlink fence, lifted her legs over, climbed a few steps down, and jumped to the ground.

"I must be insane for doing this," Lance said as he trailed behind her. "You're going to get yourself in trouble. You know, you have a habit of doing that."

She motioned for him to be quiet as she hid behind a tree. The large trunk made a great hiding place. She flitted from tree to tree until she was as close as she could get without being detected. She narrowed in on the barrels with a large red "X" marked on them, and then on the men wearing protective suits. She felt a thrill when one took his helmet off. As she clicked the sequence of pictures, the camera made a whizzing sound like a pesky horsefly buzzing around someone's head.

"Come on," Lance said. "Let's go. We're trespassing."

"Darn right you are!"

They both whirled around. Stacey was stunned; she never heard the men coming. Two men approached, one pointing a shotgun at them. "Put your hands up."

"We were just leaving," Stacey said, and took a step in the direction of the fence.

A click of the gun made her freeze.

"You're not going anywhere." The gunman held his hand out, palm up. "I'll relieve you of that camera. Now, throw it over here, nice and easy."

Reluctantly, Stacey tossed it to the two men.

"Let's move." The gunman jerked the tip of the gun in the direction of the plant. Halfway to the plant they reached a shed-sized building. The younger of the two men opened the door and flipped a switch, which turned a light on outside of the building.

He shoved them inside and tied Stacey's hands behind her back first, then Lance's. He bound their feet next. "Press your backs against each other." Winding a rope around their midsections, he gave a yank to secure the knot. "That ought to do it." As the men walked to the door, the younger one flipped the light off and said, "The boss ain't gonna like this."

Suddenly, the door slammed shut. Except for the moonlight streaming in the only window on one side of the building, they were engulfed in darkness. A chill ran over Stacey's skin.

"Well, this is another fine mess you've gotten us into," Lance said.

"You didn't exactly do anything to stop them from putting us in here."

"What did you expect me to do? That man was pointing a double-barreled shotgun at my chest. Sometimes the best move is no move at all."

"You could have said something."

"Like what?"

"I don't know. Like made up an excuse as to why we were here."

"Stacey," he said, as if trying his best to remain patient, "those men are in no mood to talk. What would I say anyway? 'Oh, sorry, we were just out for a leisurely stroll at one in the morning with our camera.' I'm sure they would have bought that one."

"Okay, you don't have to be sarcastic." A heavy silence rose between them, seeming to take up the rest of the space in the room. At long last she said, "What do we do now?"

"I've got a pocket knife in my back pocket. If we lie on our sides maybe you can reach in and get it."

"Why do I have to reach in?"

"I'm tied up at the moment, thanks to you."

"It's not my fault. I never asked you to come."

"And if I hadn't, you'd be sitting here all alone in the dark."

Just the thought of being in this situation by herself shot fear through her. "Okay. It's my fault. I'm sorry. I'll—"

"Don't say, 'I'll get us out of this.' " Lance exhaled a long, controlled breath. "I noticed he didn't tie your knots as tight as mine. I think you have more movement in your hands and wrists."

"Which way should we lie down?"

"My knife is in my back right pocket, so let's lie on my left, your right." As Lance pulled one way, Stacey pulled the other. His voice was filled with annoyance. "Stacey, you're moving to your left. Don't you know your right from your left?"

"I'm nervous, okay?" she said through gritted teeth. She was not only nervous, she was frightened, panicked, and, as crazy as it seemed, excited. She almost felt like Lois Lane in a *Superman* movie, except for the fact that this wasn't a movie. That fact shot streaks of terror through her. What would these men do to them? How far would the owner of this company go to keep what he was doing a secret? Murder? Maiming? Who knew?

Her fingers shook as she struggled to slip them into Lance's pocket. "Did you have to wear such tight jeans?" The heat from his body felt good on her cold hands. She wedged her fingers inside until they hit something hard. "I feel it." Her voice came out breathless as the blood coursed through her veins. She pulled and tugged until the knife came free. So relieved, she relaxed her hand.

Clank!

"What was that?" Lance asked.

"Uh, the knife."

He groaned.

Remaining on their sides, they scooted down until Lance felt the object with his fingers. He picked it up, flipped one of the blades open, and began to saw his way to freedom. As soon as he freed his hands, he sat upright, bringing Stacey with him. "Those guys weren't professionals—they didn't even check our pockets."

"They're hard-working employees, who want to keep their jobs." Stacey waited as Lance cut through the ropes to free his feet, then midsection. She felt the ropes tighten with every jerky movement he made. It seemed to take forever.

At long last he had removed all the ropes. He looked at her. "I should leave you here, or at the very least keep you tied up. It seems it's the only way to keep you out of trouble."

She wondered if he would indeed leave her there.

As Lance started to cut away at the ropes that bound her hands, voices shouted just outside the door. Lance's hands froze. Stacey held her breath and stared at the door, waiting for it to open. Her heart thudded in her chest so hard she could hear it pounding in her ears. A moment of silence passed and the footsteps outside faded before Lance resumed sawing, much faster this time.

As soon as her hands were free Stacey rubbed each wrist. A few minutes later Lance untied her feet. She stood. "Now what?"

Lance was already thinking ahead and had moved to the window, testing it to see if it would open.

"What do you suppose they use this shed for?" Stacey asked, rubbing her arms to ward off the cold.

"Obviously for nosy reporters."

She smiled, though she felt like laughing hysterically to release tension. Didn't he have anxiety racing through his veins too? She folded her arms over her chest to keep her body from shaking.

"Stand back." Using his elbow, Lance shattered the window. "I don't see anyone. Come on."

Without hesitation Stacey joined him at the window. "Hurry."

"I'm going as fast as I can," Lance said with a grunt.

She chewed on her fingernails while

Lance squeezed his large frame through the small window. She hopped up on the ledge.

"Watch out for the jagged pieces of glass," he said, and lifted her out. When he set her on her feet she fell forward into Lance's warm and steady arms. He enveloped her hand with his and whispered, "Let's go." They ran at full speed through the trees. Darkness enveloped them as the thick branches of the evergreens blocked out the moonlight.

She slowed to a walk. "I'm lost. I don't know where we are." Stacey tried to gain her bearings, but couldn't see much of anything.

"Follow me."

Stacey clung to Lance's hand as he led her through the woods. She heard the snapping of branches under their feet as they made their way deeper and deeper into the thicket of trees.

"Do you know where we're going?" she asked.

Lance didn't answer her until minutes later when he pushed back the limb of a fir tree and said, "To the road."

The moon shone bright over head, casting a wondrous, glorious light on their surroundings. "How'd you ever find this?"

Again, he didn't answer her. "I think our cars are in that direction."

They climbed over the fence and hiked a half mile down the road until they reached their vehicles. Stacey's shoulders slumped when she noticed her slashed tires.

"They got mine too," Lance said. He opened his trunk and pulled out a box and blanket, then snapped the lid shut. "Looks like we have a walk ahead of us."

"They might be looking for us." Alarm nearly strangled her, and she had to force herself to take deep breaths. She knew reporting could get dangerous, but never expected this dangerous, especially in a small town. She struggled to keep her teeth from chattering. The cold night brought chills to her skin, but it was fear that made her jaw vibrate like an electric massager.

Taking her hand, Lance didn't wait around to talk. He started out at a fast pace, and hurried down the road until he reached a field. They slipped between the barbed wire and entered an open pasture, then walked for what seemed like an hour before they reached an old barn. Flipping open the box he'd brought, Lance pulled out a flashlight. Scattered raindrops began to fall.

"You had a flashlight all this time and didn't use it?"

"If someone's following us they would have spotted the light from far away, right?"

"I guess."

"We're safer this way."

As Lance opened the barn door, its hinges creaked in protest from years of neglect. "Let's get inside before it pours."

Stacey tailed Lance inside. She not only didn't want to get wet, but she didn't want to be in sight if the men from Minor Chemical Company were looking for them.

The barn smelled musty, and seemed almost too quiet. Lance flashed the light on a pile of hay that lay in the center of the barn. "That's our bed for the night."

Stacey made a face. "Aren't there rats nesting in there?"

"Probably mice, but they won't eat much."

"Very funny." Her head jerked toward the rafters when she heard a flapping noise. "I hope that was a bird."

"I think it's a bat. There's probably a dozen or so up there."

Stacey swallowed. Was he trying to scare her? Because he was doing a great job. She followed him over to the haystack. Suddenly the rain unleashed its fury, thundering down on the barn. In a corner of the barn, the rain fell in a steady stream to the dirt floor.

She waited for Lance to sit down first, and hesitated before she sat down next to him. The warmth of his body felt comforting, soothing . . . and disturbing. She needed something to take her mind off of his nearness, and the comfort she felt every time he held her in his arms. "What else do you have in that box?" As she took the flashlight from him she noticed blood dripping from his hand.

"You're hurt."

"It's not bad," he said, as if he'd merely scratched himself.

Stacey took his hand in hers, flashed the light on the wound, and examined it. She turned her attention to the red and white box and opened it. "First aid kit—that's a good thing to have in your car," she said.

"Here, hold the flashlight." She unlatched the lid and took out gauze, an antiseptic pad, and a large bandage. He didn't resist when she cleaned his wound and bandaged it up.

"You're good at that," he said.

She met his eyes for a moment, smiled, then put the used material back in the box. "Think so, huh?"

"Yes. Just like I think you'd make a good mother."

"What makes you say that?"

"Because you're loving, caring, and giving. All the qualities that make a good mother—and a good wife." Before she could respond he lowered his head and captured her lips with his. He didn't give her time to think. He didn't give her time to react.

As he deepened the kiss Stacey's muscles relaxed. Slowly he lowered her onto her back. She breathed in the rich scent of his cologne mixed with the smell of hay. The sound of rain faded and the heat from his body warmed her. Despite the current danger, Stacey never felt safer. She was in the arms of the man she loved. The realization nearly brought her upright, but she quickly pushed it to the back of her mind.

Their kiss felt natural, as if they had kissed a million times before. She nestled into the straw. A smile creased her lips when Lance snuggled with her. As Stacey lay in his arms she closed her eyes. A sense of peace flowed over her, an odd feeling given their circumstance. They held each other. Neither one said a word.

Lance kissed the top of her head and in a whisper barely audible said, "I love you."

He never knew what contentment meant until now. She needed him. He couldn't recall a time when someone actually needed him for something other than money. Giving to and loving each other was a new experience for him, and he liked it.

She not only stirred his desire, but she made him feel complete, like two halves making a whole, two hearts loving as one. With Stacey by his side, he could conquer the world.

No woman had ever captured his heart the way Stacey had. A mere touch and he was completely hers. Did she have any idea how she affected him?

He had found a piece of heaven. The only problem was, would he be able to let her go if that's what she wanted? He had never been a possessive man . . . quite the opposite. But then he had never known true love before, either. The thought frightened him, another first. He closed his eyes and dropped a kiss on the side of her head.

Lance held her tight, listening to the sounds of the rain, the creek of the barn, the whistling of the wind . . . and the beat of their hearts.

Chapter Seven

Stacey slept better than she had in years, and didn't wake until Lance moved away. The cold air immediately settled on her body, sending a shiver through her. Sunlight streamed through the cracks in the barn walls, and birds chirped outside.

"We should get moving. The men at the chemical plant are sure to have noticed us missing by now," Lance said.

Stacy needed no further urging and sprang to her feet. She followed on Lance's heels across the yard until they reached the paved road.

He slipped his hand into hers, gave a

deep sigh, and said, "Looks like we have a walk ahead of us."

As they headed down the deserted road Stacey remained quiet as last night lingered in her thoughts. She couldn't believe the situation she had put him in, even before they met. First the nasty newspaper articles, then hiring him to pose as her husband, and now having their lives threatened over a story she insisted on exposing.

What was wrong with her? She had always prided herself on her intelligence. Yet in the last few weeks she had acted like an airhead.

She darted a glance at Lance, his cheeks rosy from the cold weather. He seemed so dependable, forthright, and honest. Part of her wanted to give in to his crazy idea and try to make this marriage work. Then another part of her wanted to push him away, like she had since they met.

She knew that having a relationship didn't mean her freedom and career would be sacrificed . . . somehow she just couldn't convince herself of that. Her entire life she had resisted getting close to men. She saw them as a threat, that they would eventually run her life, just as her father had. She didn't want that. She wanted a man to treat her as an equal in a partnership, someone who respected her decisions.

Of course, lately, her decisions had been made with such poor judgment they didn't deserve respect. Yet, here Lance was, walking beside her down this lonely road, and he never once criticized her choices.

Up to now no man had been worth the risk. Lance would be. That knowledge scared her.

She couldn't seem to shake the notion that Lance might be using her, but this wasn't the first time she'd questioned a man's intentions. With every date she wondered about their motives. And with Lance in the same business—a competitor, no less—he could easily be after much more than her love and affection. How could she know for sure if he really loved her for her, and not for her father's money, power, and position?

"You're sure quiet," Lance said, grinning when he glanced at her.

"I'm thinking about my story." She couldn't meet his eyes.

"Is that it?" The tone of his voice indicated he didn't believe her. "I'm sure it'll be great. All of your articles are."

She looked at him straight in the eye, this time. "Do you really think so?"

"Yes. But I have to admit I don't like to be the one you write about."

She smiled.

A car appeared in the distance. Stacey squeezed Lance's hand. "Do you think that's the men from the chemical plant?"

"I don't know." Lance focused on the car as he spoke. The expensive black sedan slowed as it neared them. "Let me do the talking."

Stacey didn't argue. The last thing she wanted to do was drum up excuses for them. Lately, she had a knack for saying the wrong thing.

The sedan stopped opposite them on the road. Because of the tinted windows they couldn't see in, giving them no clue who sat behind the driver's seat. The window hummed as it lowered.

Stacey didn't recognize the older gentleman, who was nicely dressed in a black suit, white shirt, and black and silver tie. His gray hair had streaks of white in it.

"What's the problem?" he asked.

"Our car broke down a few miles back," Lance said.

The man nodded his head in understanding. "Want a lift into town?"

"We'd really appreciate it." Needing no further persuasion, Lance opened the back door and quickly scanned the empty car before he allowed Stacey to get in first. He followed.

As the man turned the car around he said, "I'm Jacob Minor."

Stacey's eyes widened at Lance. Jacob Minor owned the chemical company. Her heart beat faster. By sheer will she steadied her breathing.

Lance gave her a stern look to keep quiet. "My name's Randolph Owens, and this is my wife, Stacey."

"What brings you way out into the country?" Jacob asked.

"I own a computer company. We were looking for a place to expand."

Jacob glanced at them in his rear view mirror. "I've heard of you through the paper."

Lance expelled a bitter laugh. "Well, don't believe everything you read."

"Don't I know it," Jacob said. "That darn

female reporter attacks everyone in the paper—me included."

Stacey struggled to keep the red from rising in her cheeks. She really didn't understand why they were bashing her when she only sought out the truth, which both men refused to give her.

As the men conversed about the pros and cons of building out in the country, her mind wandered.

When it came to relationships, Stacey had learned many times that few people wanted her friendship for its own sake. Many men, especially the ones who worked for her father, dated her in hopes of gaining a notch up the corporate ladder. She found it easy to eliminate these people from her life, but it left her with very few friends she could trust.

Perhaps that's why her family was so close-knit. They had to be. Wealth brought power. Power brought out the ambitious, the money-hungry, and those who wanted to be given money and prestige rather than work for it.

She had buried that need to be loved long ago, but now, since meeting Lance, it had resurfaced. Marc's words about Lance entered her thoughts too many times, giving her doubts and insecurities. Yet she knew that Marc was no better. He might love her, in his own twisted way, but he also wanted her father's company. And he still did.

"Here we go," Jacob Minor said.

Stacey snapped out of her thoughts as the car pulled up their driveway and stopped. After Lance thanked Jacob for the ride, they got out of the car and waved goodbye. They watched the sedan pull away, then stop and back up. Glancing at Lance, she met his questioning stare.

Jacob rolled the window down and said, "Did one of you drop this?" He held out a roll of film.

Stacey patted her back pocket, then briefly closed her eyes.

Lance was the first to find his voice and said, "Yes. Thank you." He took the film and slipped it in his pocket and waved as the sedan drove away. He looked at Stacey, his expression speaking volumes, and made no move to give her the film. "Let's go in and call a tow truck."

She followed him in and waited until he

finished his call, then used the phone to call the office.

"Stacey, where the heck have you been?" Kyle said with irritation in his voice.

"You wouldn't believe me if I told you."

"Try me."

She sighed and said, "I went to Minor Chemical Company last night to photograph them illegally dumping waste into the Lewis River. I, uh, got caught."

"You what?" Kyle's tone had real concern in it. "Did they hurt you?"

"They slashed the tires on my car, but I managed to escape. I just got home." She omitted the rest of the story—at least for now. "I'm going to work on the story at home. I'll try to be in tomorrow after I get the pictures developed."

"You still have the pictures?" Amazement was obvious in Kyle's voice.

"Call it dumb luck, but yeah."

"Also, when you get in we need to talk. I've been getting a lot of complaints about our lack of coverage on Randolph Owens. I want to get a story out on him this week."

Stacey rolled her eyes skyward, wishing he would lay off on that subject. She hung the phone up and climbed the stairs to her bedroom. After she showered and changed, she found Lance in the kitchen, eating.

"I made some scrambled eggs and toast," he said.

"I need to get my story written," she said. "Can I use your computer?"

He nodded. A loud engine could be heard outside. "The tow truck must be here. I'm going to ride with him so I can be sure to get my tires replaced."

"He's going to pick up my car too, isn't he?"

As if he hadn't considered it until now, Lance frowned before he said, "Sure."

Just before he headed out the door she ran after him. "Could you drop the roll of film to be developed while you're in town?"

Lance stared at her a moment. "Only if you promise me you'll never put yourself in danger like that again."

"I'll give you a definite maybe."

"Sorry, not good enough."

She sighed.

When she wouldn't give in, he rubbed his forehead in frustration, and walked out the door. Stacey stood in the doorway and watched him climb into the cab of the tow truck and ride away. A warmth spread through her limbs. Suddenly she couldn't wait until he returned home. She shook her head as if to rid herself of the feeling, then shut the door and returned to the kitchen.

After she ate she settled down at the computer and began to write her story about Minor Chemical Company. A bit of guilt nagged at her. Jacob Minor had been kind to them, helped them when they were in need, and now she was writing a story that could possibly throw him in jail or shut his company down. This was the side of reporting that Stacey didn't like. Sometimes nice people did bad things that had to be corrected, and this was one of those times.

Two hours later she finished the article, printed it out, and cleared the screen. She had one more article to write, one she dreaded. With a deep sigh, she tapped her finger on the arm of the chair. What could she say about Randolph Owens? Stacey decided to keep it simple, to keep the focus on his computer business. No matter how hard she tried to sensationalize the article, she knew Kyle wouldn't be happy with it, because it didn't include information about Lance's sudden marriage.

Somehow she would have to avoid that subject, at least long enough to buy her more time.

The next day Stacey asked Lance to drive her to the edge of town and drop her off so she could walk the rest of the way to work. She didn't want anyone to see her with Lance and begin asking questions. Lance had had her car towed to the garage to get new tires, and she figured the job wouldn't be done until the end of the work day.

She waited until Lance drove away before she walked into town. She entered her office right on time, took her coat off, and stepped into Kyle's office. She handed him the two articles, and returned to her desk. Only a few minutes lapsed before he called her back into his office.

"What's this?" Kyle held the paper up in the air between his index finger and thumb.

Stacey frowned. "It's either the article about the Minor Chemical Company or Randolph Owens."

"It's about Randolph Owens," Kyle said.

"I thought you were going to get me the dirt on his marriage."

Annoyance rose in Stacey's gut. Why wouldn't he drop the subject? "Sorry, Kyle, but I was a little held up by gunpoint the other night, getting you a big story on the chemical company."

The wrinkles on his forehead softened. "I don't mean to sound ungrateful, but people in this town want gossip."

"Gossip isn't journalism."

"No, but it sells."

She placed her hands on her hips. "You'd risk the integrity of this newspaper just to sell a few more papers?"

"Yep." He didn't hesitate.

"You act as if Randolph Owens' personal life is more important than chemical waste polluting our rivers and killing the animals."

Kyle dragged in a deep breath and tilted his head back as if he'd been slapped. "Your efforts are noble, but unfortunately trash sells. The people in this town lead boring lives. They want to live vicariously through the rich and famous. Now, I'm not saying that Owens Technology possibly merging with Microland isn't big news, but we need a personal story. Randolph Owens' sudden marriage is just that. And if he married a hometown girl, that makes the locals believe in fairytales."

Stacey threw her hands up in the air. "I give up." Shaking her head, she strode to the door.

Before she left the office, Kyle said, "Stan Williams is supposed to fly into South Sound sometime today. Cover that story for me and see if you can get a quote from him. An interview would be even better—and don't forget a photograph. Do you think you can handle that?"

"No problem."

He smiled and nodded, then returned his attention to the papers on his desk.

When Stacey reached her office she closed her eyes and let out a sigh. She sat down at her desk, deep in thought. Why hadn't Lance mentioned that her father was coming in tomorrow? Did Lance even know? And why was he coming? Was the merger true?

Throughout the day Stacey's mind wandered. She had so many problems, she couldn't count them all. Her father might find out that she had lied to him about getting married; that Marc or someone was trying to make trouble for them by leaking incorrect information to the newspaper; that almost got herself and Lance killed while investigating a story. And now she not only had to interview Randolph Owens, but her father as well!

After picking up the pictures she'd taken at the chemical plant and delivering them to Kyle, she decided she would leave an hour early and get her car. As she slid her coat on and removed her purse from her desk drawer, Kyle approached.

"I gave your article on the chemical plant to a few public officials. They are very interested in seeing your photos, and said they would look into the matter."

"What do you think will happen to the plant?" Stacey asked.

Kyle shrugged as if he really didn't care. "Probably get slapped with a hefty fine and monitored." He made a move to leave, then checked himself. "Oh, I thought you should know: when Wanda returns I'm putting her on the story," he said.

"The merger story?" Stacey crossed her arms over her chest, her stare narrowing on Kyle.

"No. Randolph Owens' marriage."

"I started on the story. I should finish it."

"No. I wouldn't want to cheapen your integrity." Kyle's sarcasm came across loud and clear.

"When's Wanda returning?"

"Her vacation was cut short. I called her an hour ago." Kyle strode back into his office, the decision final.

Great. Just what Stacey didn't need was a busybody like Wanda snooping around her house snapping pictures. She should warn Lance. Stacey sat back down in her chair and dialed home. Busy. She tried again. Darn. Lance must be tying up the phone with his computer. Unfortunately, at the moment, they only had one phone line.

She hurried out of the building and jogged down four blocks. Her breathing was labored by the time she reached the garage and hustled inside.

"Excuse me," Stacey said. "I'm in a hurry."

The mechanic took his time sliding out from underneath a battered brown pickup truck. He wiped his hands on a black oil-stained rag, rubbed his fingers over his thick gray mustache, and said, "What can I do for you?"

"I'm Stacey Williams . . . I mean Stacey Owens. You replaced the tires on my car." She crossed her arms and tapped her index finger. With effort, she waited.

He scratched his head, his thick eyebrows coming together. "Let me look for your papers in the office."

She followed him into a cramped room, the desk and file cabinets taking up most of the space. He rustled through the papers covering the desk. "Sorry, your car wasn't towed here. We were instructed to haul it over to the wrecking yard."

Did she hear him right? Her mouth wavered before she found her voice. "Who authorized that?"

He glanced back into the papers and read the name. "Lance Owens."

Her hands fisted into tight balls as she stormed out of the shop. Lance had better have a good explanation for this. Now how was she supposed to get home? She hastened back to the office, hoping she would find a ride. The few people in the office weren't leaving work for at least another hour, and that was too long for her to wait.

She knew that the minute Wanda got the call from Kyle she would be on her way to their home.

She headed to the front door of the office, wondering what to do now.

"I'll give you a lift home," a paper delivery boy in his early teens offered.

She was desperate, and would take a ride home with anyone right now—even a paperboy and his mother. She followed him outside to the curb and glanced at the many cars parked along the street. "Which one's yours?"

The boy frowned and jerked his head toward the building. A shiny red dirt bike was parked close to the building. "Hop on the back."

"Do you have a license to drive this thing?" she asked.

"I'm supposed to ride it off-road, but it sure beats pedaling a bicycle." He grinned and displayed the braces on his teeth.

What choice did she have? Anything would be faster than walking. She hiked up her skirt, straddled the seat, and grasped the boy's jacket. With a sudden jerk they sped off the sidewalk, thudding onto the asphalt road. He whizzed through the intersection, a van barely missing them.

Stacey closed her eyes, not wanting to see the car squash them like bugs on a windshield, and heaved a sigh of relief when they escaped out of town unharmed.

"Are you sure you should be driving this thing?" she yelled, her grip turning her knuckles white.

He looked over his shoulder and his straight sandy brown hair flew in his eyes from the wind. He wore a lopsided grin and a mischievous twinkle in his eyes. "Don't worry. I race dirt bikes. Besides, the cops haven't caught me yet."

As if that knowledge made her feel any safer. Stacey gave him directions, until they finally reached the top of her driveway.

"I'll walk from here. Thanks." She got off the bike.

With a nod and a wave, the kid drove off.

Stacey moved down the long driveway. As the house came into sight she spotted Wanda walking the premises as if she owned the place. Stacey slipped behind a thick maple tree trunk and watched. Wanda's camera clicked pictures of the house and surrounding area in rapid succession. She peered in the front window before knocking on the door. As soon as Lance answered, lightbulbs flashed in his face. He raised his hand and spoke a few words before he started to shut the door.

Wanda stuck her foot in the way. "Please, Mr. Owens. I just want a moment of your time. Who did you marry? A local woman, or someone from California? Was this planned or a spur of the moment wedding? Is your wife home? Can I speak with her?"

"Get off my property before I call the police," Lance said.

"Mr. Owens, if you'll answer just one of my questions I'll leave," Wanda said.

Lance paused.

"What is Mrs. Owens' name?"

Stacey held her breath. Her heart thudded. If Lance revealed who she was, she'd have Wanda chasing after her with dozens of questions.

"Why is my personal life so interesting to you? I moved to a small town to get away from people. But it seems I had more privacy in L.A., among the millions of people who live there."

"You're the most famous person we've ever had live here. Oh, except for that time Bing Crosby stopped for a visit."

"I can't imagine why he left," Lance said sarcastically. "Besides, you've got the wrong Randolph Owens. My father is the developer, not me."

"Really?" Wanda tilted her head.

"Yes. Really."

"I heard you were merging with Microland."

"Not that I know of. Now if you'll excuse me." Lance glanced between Wanda's foot and her face.

"Oh. Of course." She hastily turned and waddled to her car. Stacey held her breath as the woman passed her. She remained where she was until Wanda's car disappeared from sight. Then Stacey traveled the remainder of the driveway and unlocked the front door. Entering the house, she ambled into the living room, suddenly very tired.

"Lance," she called out.

Stacey had to wait several minutes before he came out of his office. She folded her arms over her chest and glared at him.

"What gave you the right to have my car towed to the wrecking yard?"

"It wasn't dependable so I bought you another one. It should be delivered within the hour. I was going to drive it over to pick you up from work." He glanced at his watch. "Aren't you home early?"

She didn't tell him that the reason she left work early was to intercept Wanda. She stuck to the issue. "You should have asked me about the car."

"You can thank me later," Lance said. "I'm busy now."

"*Thank* you?" Her brows creased together. "I'm not thanking you. You had no right doing anything with my car."

"I don't understand why you're getting so upset about this." He pivoted to walk away.

"Because it was *my* car. I should have the final say about it. If I needed a new one I would have bought one."

As if she tested his patience, he slowly turned to look at her and paused. "You're overreacting."

"And you're too controlling. You're not my father."

Lance whirled around, his glare narrowing. "I don't want to be your father. I want to be your husband, and part of a husband's job is to take care of his wife." He drew in a deep breath and exhaled, calming himself.

"Don't you think you're taking your job a little too seriously?"

"This is not a good time to have this discussion."

"Seems like the perfect time to me." She lifted her hands in the air, then let them smack on her sides. "I can take care of myself. I don't need your help."

"You did the other night. You put yourself in a lot of danger investigating the chemical plant."

"I agree," Stan said, coming into the room. "Lance told me all about your investigative reporting. Stacey, that's too dangerous for a woman."

For a moment she stared at her father, shocked to see him there, and even more surprised that Lance hadn't told her. She struggled to find her voice. "Dad. What are you doing here?"

"I had something I needed to discuss with Lance."

"It must be serious for you not to have

handled it over the phone?" She stepped over to him and kissed him on the cheek, noting his pale complexion and the dark circles under his eyes.

"Nothing for you to worry about. I just wanted to discuss something with Lance in person."

"Discuss what?"

"Business."

Stacey knew from past experience that her father's clipped answer meant it was none of her business. "Did Mom come?"

"No, she couldn't make it. But she wanted me to give you her love."

Stacey smiled.

"And," Stan continued, "your sisters wanted me to tell you that they plan on coming down soon to see your new house."

This time Stacey had to force a smile. Faith might want to see her new house, but her real reason would be to see how Stacey's "arrangement" was going.

"Would you like to stay for dinner?" Stacey asked.

"No thanks. I have a lot to do before my surgery."

"You scheduled your surgery? That's

great." A sense of relief swept through Stacey.

"Actually I haven't scheduled it yet. I plan to do that today."

"The doctor will happy to hear that."

"I can see your mother's been talking to you about it."

"She worries about you, Dad. We all do."

"Well, I was beginning to worry myself. But now that I have another man I can depend on, I feel much better about everything." Stan smiled over at Lance, but Lance didn't return the gesture. Instead he watched for Stacey's reaction.

Why did she have a feeling she wasn't going to like what her father meant by his statement?

"I've got to get going," Stan said. "I have a helicopter waiting for me at the airstrip. Could you give me a ride, Lance?"

"Of course." Lance addressed Stacey. "When the delivery man gets here with your car, all you have to do is sign for it." He swept his arm wide, gesturing for Stan to lead the way out the door.

"Dad."

Stan paused with his hand on the door handle, and turned to look back at Stacey.

"Be sure and let me know when you're going to have your operation."

He nodded, then left the house with Lance behind him.

Stacey stepped over to the window and watched both men get in the car and drive away. Shouldn't *she* be the one taking her father to the airport, and not her temporary husband? But it wasn't possible—her car had been retired to the car graveyard. Lance sure had moved into her family's life in a hurry.

She watched the sun struggling to peek out from behind a stratus cloud. A gust of wind blew the remaining dangling maple leaves, doing its best to make them fall. Maybe she should be grateful to Lance. He'd been able to get her father to make an appointment with the surgeon, which no one else in the family was able to do.

Stacey couldn't help but wonder how her father would react when Lance finally left, and the truth came out. Her heart grew heavy at the thought. What she should be wondering was how *she* would react when he left.

She smiled as an image of Lance appeared in her mind. His good looks, charming personality, and gentle nature drew her to him like a magnet. She enjoyed his company, even longed for it on bad days. He always knew the right thing to say to cheer her up. They shared their ideas, and he really listened and respected what she suggested. He had even come to her the other night and asked her to help him troubleshoot another computer programming error. She liked helping him.

And when they occasionally touched, her heart flip-flopped. He had the sweetest kisses, and gave the greatest shoulder massages. So many times she'd wanted to give in to him, but something held her back. If she could just figure out what that was, their marriage could stand a chance. Until then, he would remain her best friend, because that's what he had become.

Chapter Eight

Stacey smelled the coffee brewing before she descended the stairs. Lance might not be the best cook in the world, but he sure brewed delicious coffee. She skipped down the stairs, in a better mood than she had been in weeks. With her father's surgery scheduled soon, that took one less worry off her list. He would be fine. She just knew it.

Entering the kitchen she spotted Lance sitting at the breakfast table, a cup of coffee in hand, reading the newspaper.

"Good morning," Stacey said. When he didn't reply, she said, "Everything okay?"

"No." He glared at her.

She frowned. "What? What's wrong?" Her heart began to pound in her chest.

"How could you do this?"

Stacey relaxed. "Oh. You mean the article I wrote about you. Well, I tried to keep it tame and focused on your computer business. I thought it might even help."

Lance's expression never changed. "I'm not talking about the article about me. I'm talking about the article you wrote about your father." He pushed out of his chair, the newspaper crumpled in his fist. "I can't believe you'd stoop so low."

Her mouth wavered. Instead of saying something she took the paper from him and glanced at the front page headline that read, "Stan Williams' Mysterious Illness."

"Oh my gosh," Stacey said, her glance meeting Lance's. "I didn't write this."

"Your name's on it."

"I swear to you I never wrote this. How could you believe I'd do something like this? We're talking about my father."

"Darn right you're talking about your father."

"Oh no," she said with a groan, and rubbed her forehead. "Kyle's source must have sent him this information."

"Source? You mean Marc, your old *boy-friend*." Lance made boyfriend sound like a dirty word. "I'm going to sue that newspaper, and your friend, Marc Newell."

Talking more to herself than to Lance, Stacey said, "I can't believe Marc would do something like this." Her mind whirled with options. "Look, I'll get Kyle to write a retraction, okay?"

The scowl on Lance's face softened, but his lips remained clamped.

"You're getting awfully defensive over a man you just met," Stacey said.

"I happen to like and respect your father. He has made me realize just how important family is, and how nice it is to have someone around you can depend on."

Her lips curved up. She studied his face, aware of the fact that that was how she felt about him. "Yeah. I know what you mean."

He tilted his head, a puzzled expression crossing his face.

Before he could answer she said, "I'd better get to work before everyone else does, so I can have a talk with Kyle in private."

"I hope you have success, because if you don't, Kyle will have to deal with me."

*   *   *

Stacey stormed into the newspaper office and went directly into Kyle's office, slamming the door behind her.

Kyle looked up in surprise.

Stacey tossed the newspaper article in front of him. "I didn't write this. Why'd you put my name on it?"

"We used a lot of your information, so I thought I'd give you the credit."

"Credit? For what? You speculated on whether my father had AIDS or not. How could you do such a thing?"

"Your father? Stan Williams—" As if suddenly making the connection he said, "I never would have guessed he was your father."

"Well, he is. And I want to know where you get off making such accusations."

Kyle's bushy brows came together. "I had a reliable source."

"This reliable source doesn't happen to be Marc Newell, does it?" Kyle's shocked expression told her all she needed to know. She lowered her voice, and took a breath to calm down. "It's bad enough you sent that snoopy woman around my home, asking my husband personal questions. But when you attack my father like this, that's the bottom line. This newspaper is nothing more than a gossip magazine. I'll have no part of it. I quit."

Stacey strode to the door and whipped it open. She could hear Kyle calling her back and saying, "Your husband? Are you saying *you're* the woman who married Owens? Stacey, come back here!"

When she slammed the outside door to the newspaper office, she felt as if a ton of bricks had just fallen off her shoulders. Relief rushed over her like coming in to a warm house after being in a blizzard.

Her next stop: Seattle.

Stacey climbed into her brand-new car. She loved the smell of the leather seats and the shine on the dashboard. Lance had selected a blue luxury vehicle. The color of the car reminded her of his eyes.

As she drove out of town, she used the phone Lance had had installed in the car. He hadn't forgotten anything. Instead of getting Lance, the message machine picked up. "Lance, this is Stacey. I'm going up to Seattle and won't be back until this evening. See you then."

She hung the phone up before she accelerated onto the freeway. She had to admit—she really loved her new car.

Stacey parked in a visitor's parking slot at her father's business. She'd had no problem getting through the security gate, the guard having known her for years. After she climbed out of the car and locked it, she made the long walk from the parking lot into the building. Her feet already ached, and she hadn't even reached the elevators yet. She loved the teal blue suit she was wearing, but the matching shoes always hurt her feet.

By the time she reached the fifth floor, Stacey struggled to control her temper. She barged into Marc's office, unannounced and uninvited. His secretary chased after her.

"All right, you little weasel. I know you're the one sending Kyle all those fictitious tips about Lance and my father."

"I'm sorry, Mr. Newell," his blond and curvaceous secretary said, her red lips frowning. "She just barged in before I could stop her."

Stacey didn't take her eyes off of Marc, nor did he break the stare with her as he said, "It's okay, Christine. I'll handle it."

He waited until the door clicked shut, then leaned back in his chair and clasped his hands behind his head. "Now what has you so upset, Stace?"

"It's Stacey. And don't patronize me." She jabbed her finger in the air at him. "You went too far when you started spreading lies about my father."

"I did no such thing. Besides, I wouldn't be so quick to condemn, when *you're* the one telling lies. I know the truth about you and your so-called marriage."

Her head tilted back as if he'd smacked her in the face. "I don't know what you're talking about."

Marc pushed out of his chair and came around his desk, pausing at a table. He opened a file filled with papers. "Seems there's no record of you and Owens ever getting married in Las Vegas. In fact, the only document I could find was the one you two signed the night of the wedding celebration at your parents' house." His tone was confident, cocky.

Stacey wanted to wipe the smug expression off his face. Her fingers curled into her palms. "Well, then you did sloppy research."

He wagged a finger at her. "Oh no. You know me better than that—one thing I never do is sloppy research. You see, I also found this in the *South Sound Newspaper*." He held the clipping out, but she refused to look at it. "Seems someone put an ad in the newspaper the week of the party for a temporary husband." His smile faded, his eyes took on an angry gleam, and his voice turned cold and threatening. "The ad has your desk number on it."

"Of course it does," Stacey said. "I handle some of the ads. So what?"

Marc tossed the newspaper back into the file. "Awfully coincidental. Especially when no one in the office knew who put the ad in the newspaper, and they had no paperwork on it."

"A filing error." She shrugged. "Happens all the time."

"I don't think so."

She folded her arms over her chest. "Besides, how Lance and I met is none of your business. What matters is that he is my husband and I love him."

"But the real question is, does he love you or your father's business?"

"That's ridiculous."

"Is it? Why don't you ask him?" Marc held the phone out. "He can be reached at extension four-twenty-one."

"That's my father's extension."

"I know."

Tilting her chin up, she snatched the phone from his hand and punched in the numbers. When the secretary answered Stacey said, "Hi Jeanette. This is Stacey. Hey, does my husband, Lance Owens, happen to be there?"

"Yes. You'll be able to reach him at this number from now on."

"From now on?" A knot began to form in Stacey's stomach.

"Yes, uh," Jeanette said, sounding confused. "You do know he's taking over for your father, don't you?"

Stacey quickly recovered, saying, "Of course I do."

"I'll put you through."

"Lance Owens."

Stacey sucked in a breath. "Lance, what are you doing here?"

"Stacey? Didn't you get my note?"

"What note?"

"The note I left on the kitchen table explaining everything."

"No, I didn't. I left for Seattle right after I talked with Kyle."

"Where are you?"

"In Marc's office." A dead silence hung over the line. Stacey could only hear Lance's heavy breathing.

"I'll be right there," Lance said.

"That's not necessary. I'll come to you." Slowly, she hung the phone up.

Marc wore a satisfied grin. "Now answer my question. Did he marry you for love, or for the love of your father's company?"

Stacey entered the office and stopped to stare at Lance sitting at her father's desk. He looked handsome in a black business suit, crisp white shirt, and gray silk tie. He had groomed his hair back, and was clean-shaven. She could almost smell his cologne from where she stood.

"Come in and shut the door," Lance said. His gaze never left her as she crossed the room and sat down in a chair opposite the desk. "I know what you're thinking, but you're wrong."

She said nothing.

"I wanted to tell you this morning, but you left in such a hurry I didn't have time."

"What about last night?" she said.

"I had to read up on various projects your father had talked to me about. I didn't get to bed until the early morning hours."

"You told me you wouldn't do this."

Lance glanced away for a moment, before returning his gaze to her. "Your father needed my help. I agreed to help him."

"How convenient."

He crossed his arms over his chest. "I knew you'd react this way. You think I had some master plan to take over your father's company. And I can guess who reinforced that idea into your mind."

"Is he right?"

Lance sighed. "Look, if you don't trust me, then at least trust your father's judgment in selecting me for this position."

Stacey rested her hands in her lap, and dropped her gaze to them.

Lance continued. "I'm going to be working here for a while, until your father can get back on his feet after the surgery. He's offered to let us stay with them in their Seattle condominium. So will you live here for a few weeks . . . with me?"

She expelled a sharp breath. "Moving's

not a problem since I am now unemployed. I quit my job."

Lance's eyes widened. "You did?"

"Yeah. I couldn't work for a place that bashed my father and made me write nasty articles about my husband, even if you are only a temporary husband." She met his glance to gauge his reaction.

Lance remained stoic. "You realize this means we'll be sharing a room together— again." Now it was his turn to watch her reaction.

"Not to worry. My mother has plenty of pillows."

A genuine smile creased Lance's mouth. "Okay."

She dipped her head again, feeling like their marriage had just become another business deal. "So should we shake on it?" She forced a laugh, the tension between them uncomfortable.

Lance stood and stepped around the large mahogany desk. "Sure." He extended his hand. When she slipped hers into his he gathered her into his arms. Before she could protest he lowered his mouth to hers, his kiss slow and sweet. He lifted his head, but kept their lips only inches apart. "Now

I'd say that's better then a handshake. Wouldn't you?"

His kiss left her breathless and dizzy. Sharing a bed with him this time would be much more difficult. "I, uh, better let you get back to work. I'm sure you're very busy."

"I'll see you tonight at your parents' place," he said, but didn't release his hold on her.

She nodded.

Lance briefly closed his eyes, as if he didn't want to let her go. He dragged in a deep breath and exhaled before he loosened his hold and returned to his chair.

The feel of his kiss lingered as Stacey walked away. Slowly but surely Lance had wiggled his way deeper into her life, her family's life, and her heart.

Stacey paced the waiting room at Virginia Mason Hospital for the hundredth time, it seemed. She checked her watch. Faith and Pamela had gone to lunch, but Stacey couldn't eat. Her father had been out of surgery for hours, and all she could do was wait, while feeling so helpless. She hugged her waist, and wished Lance was holding her in his arms right now. She needed his support, his strength that always assured her everything would be all right.

In the past weeks he had become a true friend to her and her family. He had been there every time she'd been in trouble, which had been many. Her heart overflowed with love for him, yet the fear and doubt still lingered in the back of her mind. Marc might have been the one to put the thought in her mind, but she was the one who kept it there.

How could she not?

Stacey had seen many people in the past try to use her to get ahead. Money and power did strange things to people. But would Lance be affected? Her heart told her no—her past experience with men told her yes.

Carol came into the waiting room, composed and collected, but Stacey detected the circles of worry under her mother's eyes even makeup couldn't cover up.

"Your father would like to speak with you," Carol said. "We just spoke with the doctor and he is very encouraged. He thinks your father will be fine."

Stacey released a long, nervous breath. "What a relief. How's he feeling?"

"Better. Just don't upset him."

Stacey nodded, then strolled down the hall. She paused at the door to his private room, put on a pleasant smile, and pushed through the door. "Hi, Dad. How are you feeling?"

"Fine." He motioned for her to come and sit beside him.

"You look good, strong." She lied.

"I wanted to talk to you alone."

"What about?"

He held his hand up to silence her. "I have some things I want to say to you, explain to you, things you should know." He hesitated before saying, "Stacey, I want you to know why I pushed you so much in your career."

"Dad, let's not get into this . . . not now."

"I need to. Now be quiet and listen."

She decided it was best to let him speak.

"I know I pushed you into programming and fought against you going into journalism and becoming a reporter. But during the short time you worked for me, I saw real genius in your work. You are so good at program development and code, I hated to see you throw that all away." He sighed. "But I know you need to do what makes you happy. So if you want a life of a newspaper reporter, then I'll be more understanding about it."

"Actually, Dad, I quit my job."

His thin white brows rose. "You did?"

"Yes, I did. Reporting didn't turn out to be as enjoyable as I thought it would be."

"So what are you going to do now?"

"I don't know." A silence rose between them, but it was one of calmness and peace, and perhaps mutual respect.

"You know I'll always be here for you if you need me."

She smiled and covered his hand with hers. "And I'll be here for you too, Dad."

Stan turned his hand over and gave hers a squeeze. "There's something else I wanted to discuss with you."

"What's that?"

"It has to do with your husband."

A knot formed in her stomach. She remained silent because at the moment she was unable to speak. Stacey released the breath she'd been holding.

"I've offered him a job."

"To take over your company," Stacey finished for him.

"No. I'm planning on expanding my business. Actually this plan has been in the works for years, and now I believe it's the right time to finally do it. I'm going to build down in the South Sound area, and I've asked Lance to run the company."

Stacey swallowed. "What did he say?"

"I was quite surprised by his reply. He said he thought you should run it."

"*Me*? I don't have any experience running a computer business."

"That's what I said." Stan studied his daughter. "He told me that if you turned the job down, then it would be up to you to make the decision whether or not he accepted my offer."

"Lance wanted me to decide? Why?"

"Don't you think that's obvious, Stacey?" Stan asked. When she gave him a questioning glance he continued. "He's afraid you'll think he married you so he could get his hands on my company." Stan shook his head. "He's not that kind of man. And I think he's proven he's a man of character and integrity. You are very lucky to have found such a gem. There's not many men like him."

A lump formed in Stacey's throat. How could she have doubted him all along? Lance was an honorable man, a good, kind, loving man, a man who truly loved her for who she was and not who her family was, or what they had. A warmth of love spread to every part of her body. She sat with her father for the next hour and held his hand as he closed his eyes and rested. They never exchanged any words, yet Stacey knew she would cherish this memory for the rest of her life.

A light knock on the door brought Stacey out of her thoughts.

Lance entered the room. "I hope I'm not interrupting."

Stan opened his eyes. In a groggy voice he said, "Not at all. Come in."

Stacey pushed out of her chair and smiled at Lance. "I guess congratulations are in order."

"Congratulations for what?"

"For being the man selected to head the South Sound Microland." She crossed the room to him, placed her hands on either side of his face, and kissed him tenderly. "Congratulations," she whispered.

"Are you sure this is what you want?" Lance asked.

"Positive. Right, Dad?" She glanced over her shoulder at him, letting her hands drop to her side. She slipped her hand into Lance's.

A wide smile broke out on Stan's face.

Stacey turned back to Lance. "So, Mr. Owens, do you know where I might be able to get a job? I'm unemployed right now, but I'm a fairly decent programmer."

"You can have any position you want, just as long as it's not a nosy reporter position," Lance said.

Stacey, Lance, and Stan all laughed.

"Maybe the best position for me right now would be a mother and wife . . . what do you think?"

"Do you mean it?" Lance asked.

"Yes I do. And the sooner the better."

"I second that," Stan said.

Lance pulled Stacey into an embrace and kissed her. "I love you," he said.

"And I love you," Stacey replied. "So, when do you want to start trying?"

"Now," Lance said without hesitation.

They laughed.

Suddenly the door burst open and Marc charged in. "Mr. Williams, I know this isn't the best time to tell you this, but someone has to disclose the truth about this phony husband." He jerked his head in Lance's direction. "He married your daughter so he could get his hands on your company. He doesn't love Stacey, not like I do."

"I think you'd better leave," Lance said, and took a step forward in Marc's direction.

"What are you thinking, Marc?" Stacey asked. "My father has just come out of surgery."

"I've got to tell your father the truth before he makes a big mistake and lets this guy head up the South Sound operations."

"Marc," Stan said, "that's already been decided."

"Have any papers been signed?" Marc asked.

"No."

"Then it's not too late." Marc stepped over to Stan and set the file folder on his lap. "Inside you'll find all my research, which documents how these two were never married in Las Vegas, and how Owens was hired by Stacey to pose as her husband. He's nothing but a two-bit actor." Marc rushed on to say, "A year ago he lost his business, and he had to start over. That's when he moved from California to South Sound. The only thing Owens owns is the name of his business, nothing more."

"That makes him an even better candidate to run my expansion, doesn't it? He won't have any other obligations to contend with," Stan said.

Marc's eyes widened and jaw dropped. "Mr. Williams, I can't let you make this huge mistake."

"Marc," Stan said, "it's time for you to leave."

"I did thorough research. I know I'm not mistaken."

Stan raised his voice. "Marc. I said leave." He pointed to the door.

Marc's nostrils flared as he glared at Stacey and Lance, then departed.

"My goodness," Stacey said. "Marc's really lost his mind. I don't know where he'd get such a crazy idea."

"Well, I think we should let your father get his rest. He looks a bit tired," Lance said, and guided Stacey to the door.

"Oh, Stacey and Lance," Stan said. "Just so you know, I did my research, too. And I'm *very* thorough." He leaned over and dumped the file into the garbage can. A smile as wide as Puget Sound appeared on Stan's face, followed by a chuckle.